CRANNÓG 45 summer 2017

Editorial Board

Sandra Bunting
Ger Burke
Jarlath Fahy
Tony O'Dwyer

GW00630735

ISSN 1649-4865
ISBN 978-1-907017-47-6

Cover image: 'Hidden' by Maeve Curtis
Cover image sourced by Sandra Bunting
Cover design by Wordsonthestreet
Published by Wordsonthestreet for Crannóg magazine
www.wordsonthestreet.com @wordsstreet

Comhairle Cathrach na Gaillimhe
Galway City Council

CONTENTS

The Galway Study Centre

Since 1983, the Galway Study Centre has been dedicating itself to giving an excellent education service to post-primary school students in Galway.

info@galwaystudycentre.ie
Tel: 091-564254

www.galwaystudycentre.ie

Submissions for Crannóg 46 open July 1ˢᵗ until July 31st
Publication date is October 27ᵗʰ 2017

Crannóg is published three times a year in spring, summer and autumn.

Submission Times: Month of November for spring issue. Month of March for summer issue.

Month of July for autumn issue.

We will <u>not read</u> submissions sent outside these times.

POETRY: *Send no more than three poems. Each poem should be under 50 lines.*

PROSE: *Send one story. Stories should be under 2,000 words.*

We do not accept postal submissions.

When emailing your submission we require **three** *things:*

1. *The text of your submission included both in body of email and as a Word attachment (this is to ensure correct layout. We may, however, change your layout to suit our publication).*

2. *A brief bio in the third person. Include this both in body and in attachment.*

3. *A postal address for contributor's copy in the event of publication.*

To learn more about Crannóg Magazine, or purchase copies of the current issue, log on to our website:

www.crannogmagazine.com

JOURNEY FROM ORLANDO, FLORIDA TO
CLARE ISLAND, CO MAYO   LINDSEY BELLOSA

Inspired by James Wright's *Lying in a Hammock at William Duffy's Farm in Pine Island, Minnesota*

The chicken hawk is looking for home.
Having left America, having flown and driven
hours and miles, landscapes are colours, impressions.
This last stretch of journey is Westport to Roonagh, then the ferry.
Clare Island on the horizon. You see the comfort of home;
I see a hump of land on sea, whale rising from water.
'The rock' the islanders say. 'Inside' they say.
An island: landscape of dreams, decided outcome.
But the chicken hawk floats and looks. The world of the island
becomes large, inside. I have seen so many places.
But each afternoon on the island becomes its own field of sunlight,
each evening darkening and blazing up again.
Time stretches into a distance you don't feel going.
The island knows this. From here, I know it too.
How far do we blow away and away, and then see:
this has been my life. All beauty in the island ...
bronze evenings of summer, deep quiet winters
and animals grazing. We are asleep in it, tucked up,
waves lapping. But from here, the whale rises up.
It will swallow our lives.

WARD 3B, LIVERPOOL WOMEN'S HOSPITAL
MARIA ISAKOVA BENNETT

Tonight, oxygen hushes through a tube.
Yes please, to a cuff, a cannula, a needle.

A green light signals morphine, slow release –
eight mls, nine mls, ten. Itchy skin.

Each breath is a small rasp
like scrunching paper. I must not turn.

Wait, wait. There's a slip toward sleep only
to trip back up again, but somewhere

beneath my ribs, promises stir –
of summer, of painting, of pages of words,

and my body remembers how to
flex my knees, sip, swallow, kiss.

COUNTRIES   ROBERT BEVERIDGE

I see you
stare like Nassau in the afternoon
your velvet look burns bright
along my arms

I touch you
as a friend, Poland in grey dusk,
Danzig's boats run low
swim for shore

I want you
more than water, Canada at the new moon
the chill of it rasps
up my empty spine

We come together
perfect Marxists in the Russian dawn
give all for country
without question

THEY TOOK TO THE SKY   CHRIS EDWARDS-PRITCHARD

The Old Lady and the Two Princesses were going out of their minds shouting my name and searching the garden with Dad's torch, which is what we still called it even though Dad popped his clogs in July. It was dawn, and there was a fair amount of cloud cover: sixty-two per cent according to my phone. The clump of trees at the bottom of the garden, where thousands of unseen starlings chirped and beeped, was backlit with an orange halo. Maya, the smaller and more annoying of the Two Princesses, screamed my name with a terrifying pitch. 'Iiiiiiiiiiiiiiaaaaaaaannn,' she said. The starlings stopped their wiry chirping, and erupted, all at once. Thousands of them, up, up, up, darting and swaying, weaving and playing, swarming as a shoal and massing into one big dark rain cloud and then dispersing like the birth of a star; curling into a question mark, a snake, a whale. And speeding under the telephone cables before errkkkkkkk, cranking the Starling Express handbrake and doubling back to perform a low swoop over our house and then morphing into some kind of flying saucer, a sausage, a spinning corkscrew. Maya and the other Princess, Gail, took shelter under the outside dining table which would usually have been tucked away in the shed by now, it being November, but that was Dad's job, and the Old Lady was too weak to haul a hulking great table. She barely had the energy to lift her lips into a smile. 'I hate them,' said Maya, 'I hate them all.' 'I hate them too,' said Gail, 'I hate them more.' The Old Lady stood in the middle of the garden in her dressing gown, her arms tucked close and hunched a little due to the low temperature, which was two point five degrees according to my phone. I watched her watch the starlings. Her eyes sketched the contours of their flow, squinting a little as they dashed away and widening as they swelled overhead, then her brow furrowed as a small watery pellet of starling poo found its mark on her shoulder, and splattered onto her neck. I laughed, and so surrendered the location of my top secret hiding place on the roof of the shed. She sighed, and did a weird mini-shake of her Old Lady head and spoke in the direction of the shed. 'It's not funny, Ian,' she said, 'do you realise how cold it is out here?' I waited a second or two. Some of the starlings were already returning to their roost. The fatter ones, the children, those with respiratory conditions. I said, 'Yes, its two point five degrees according to my phone.'

The starlings did that every morning from early November onwards. It was called a murmuration. Which was a problem because I often had difficulty with saying long words such a murmuration. I had no problem thinking them, just saying them. Mur-mur-muration, I would sometimes say. And the Two Evil Princesses would tease me: mur mur mooor meer mur murrrr moooooooration. The Old Lady would tell them that if they had nothing pleasant to say, then they should say nothing at all and hurry along and eat up all of that asparagus, please, it's not cheap. The Old Lady had become pretty lacklustre at discipline since Dad pegged it. She lacked conviction, and follow-through. Take the morning she caught me on top of the shed – she said nothing, absolutely nothing, as I stormed inside and up to my room. Hours later she brought me a steaming mug of hot chocolate and asked if I was okay, sitting beside me and brushing my hair to one side. I mean really! What a pushover. What a chump! 'Are you okay, Ian?' What a dupe! What a fool! I said that I was fine. I told her I just wanted to know why the starlings did what they did. 'Why do they fly like that?' I asked her. She said that as far as she knew there was no explanation for a murmuration, but her personal theory was that they were displaying safety in numbers to ward off predators, like buzzards. 'You're wrong,' I said, 'it's much more magical than that.' She laughed and made me promise to watch them from my window the next morning, and kissed me on the forehead, which was a bit gross but not entirely unwelcome.

The next morning I hopped out of bed and straight into Dad's old mountaineering shoes. They were too big so I wore quadruple layers of socks. It was ten minutes until sunrise and, pressing my ear against the window, I could already hear the starlings chattering. The sky was a deep dark blue and it looked a little drizzly out there. My phone had predicted sleet, but it didn't look much like sleet. I crept downstairs and made my way into the kitchen. I could tell straight away that the Old Lady had hidden the keys to the back door as all of the keys had gone from the key jar, and the window keys, which usually lived on a shelf in front of cookbooks, were also missing. Wily Old Lady. But little did she realise that I knew the whereabouts of the spare back door key. Aha! I lifted the cookie jar and found ... a note. Not a key, but a note. Written in green glitter. It read: go back to bed, stupid. With back spelt bee ayy kay, and stupid with an ooooooh instead of a ewe. It was the Two Princesses. How dare they! I searched the rest of the kitchen but there was soon the sound of a large wave crashing upon a shore, muffled, as if heard from a beach hut. It was the starlings. I rushed to the window and watched them flush into the sky and become lost for a second in the moody clouds before darting out beyond the window frame. Goodbye, friends. There was a creak in the floorboard. My two sisters emerged from the shadows, their arms linked. 'What do you think you're doing?' said Maya. I told her to go away. 'Why are you so in love with the birds?' asked Gail. I said, 'I'm just interested in why they do what they do.' 'We think you want to marry them,' said Gail, 'and have babies.' They giggled. And started singing: 'Iiiian and the birdies sitting in the tree k-i-s-s-i-n-g.' I told them to shut up and if necessary shove their irritating little songs up their smelly bottoms. They didn't like that. They retaliated by launching themselves at me, the ugly little Princess goblins with faces smothered in puckered pustules and oozy warts, and festering matted hair all down their arms right to the tip of shattered yellow nails. I opened the cutlery drawer and tried to fend them off with a handful of spoons. Back, you cretins. Back to the swamps on which you were spawned. But they clawed my skin and yanked my hair so I was pretty relieved to see the Old Lady's feet plunking down the stairs and her hands forming barriers between myself and the demented duo. I told the Old Lady that she really needed to get a handle on her parenting skills as the Two Princesses were completely out of control. 'Okay, Ian,' she said. And then I said, 'If Dad were still here none of this would be happening.' That stopped all three of them in their tracks. The Two Princesses were in shock, mouths silenced and agape, and the Old Lady stood very still for a moment but chose to handle the situation with affection, rather than anger, which is something she was really good at. She knelt to my level and gave me a hug and beckoned for the twins to join in, which they did.

The Old Lady told me that she would return both sets of back door keys to the kitchen because I was the oldest child and she trusted me to show a little self-restraint and act as a good role model for the twirpy Princesses. 'Be more like your father,' she said. Hoping that that would have sufficient emotional clout. Yes, Old Lady. Of course, Old Lady. The next morning I was outside ten minutes before sunrise. It was a crisp, calm morning. Not a cloud in the sky. I dodged the snails that were slowly sloping along the garden path and I climbed the ladder to the roof of the shed. Finally I was alone. Dad used to sit up there with me all the time. We used to watch the stars. I would identify them using the Star Tracker app on my phone and Dad would tell me about UFOs and Martians and intergalactic travel. He told me that the Two Princesses were most likely beings from outer space and denied any involvement in their creation. Outcasts, he said. Banished from a distant realm for tripping up their alien Grandma with their alien skipping rope. I waited for the starlings. Eventually, and with a sudden whoosh, they took to the sky. Hundreds and hundreds of black-blue specks shooting upwards and then in one synchronised movement chicaning back down and whipping over the canopy of oak and elder before hanging in the mid-air and shape-shifting into a balloon, a bloated jellyfish, a wingless aeroplane, and so on. I implored them. I conducted them. 'Faster, faster,' I said, with my arms aloof. I spun around on the shed-top and above me they whisked through the sky, spiralling into a great tornado which turned and churned and funnelled its way towards me. 'Why do you do this?' I shouted. And they hovered closer and closer. I had to really steady myself for a moment and then like a sudden onslaught of rain I was in the eye of the starling storm, fully surrounded by a spinning wall of wings. They grabbed my coat with their beaks and in one swoop picked me up and lifted me from the shed. I was flying. I was one of them now. We flashed into the sky at a great speed, myself at the heart of the Starling Machine, inside the feathered cockpit whose walls were constantly vanishing and replenishing – one group splintering away and another immediately filling the gap. Such a thing could not be rehearsed. It was intuition, impulse. We dipped, we soared, we undulated and we created art all over the breaking of a new day – the simmering fuzz of a morning murmuration. Suddenly, one of the starlings was knocked backwards from the flock by some kind of object, a projectile, and I was flung to the front. Sure enough, there were the Two Princesses at the foot of the Old Lady's rockery, gathering stones and lobbing them at the flock, trying to bring it down. 'Die, you stupid things,' said Maya. We turned in an instant and dived at the little rascals, roaring like a freight train over their stupid heads, which they covered with their arms, screaming. And then, a new sound presented itself to the mad cacophony. The sound of laughter. It was the Old Lady from her bedroom window, her eyes full of wonder and her head tilted to one side and her arms dangling the way Maya and Gail dangle when they are watching a firework display. The Old Lady was laughing her tonsils out, the red little cowbells going two to the dozen. She laughed, and the Two Princesses screamed, and I, at the very heart of the murmuration, finally understood why the birds did what they did: to fly, to be free, to screech and tumble through the universe, and never, ever, deny the simple beauty of impulse.

THE SPACE BETWEEN US   LINDA OPYR

Blind as a star, deaf
as a sun, we love.

A woman in a cold land searches
for her eyes in the mirror, asks
What if?

In a city where morning rattles like a snake, a man
smells hot tar being spread, closes his window, vows
Never Again.

And before the deepening shade grows into night,
somewhere a shadow raises a pen in a blue whisper
over the empty wine glass of a page,
We can.

Young, I could name the planets, thought
I knew them all. Yet I could not have imagined,
there where no one had ever looked, you.

Nameless beyond the majestic spin of your distance,
your silent pull at the space between us.

SYNESTHESIA   BRUCE BOSTON

Shadow lines of night
close on the horizon,
slicing the last sounds of light
to strips so thin
they are ultrasonic,

like finely hammered
gold leaf
pressed
to the thickness of a single atom,
so thin they are transparent
to the inner ear
in the yellow lamps of dusk,

so thin you
can almost hear
their translucent shades,
taste their fragrance
on the tines of tomorrow.

BEYOND THE PALE   PETER BRANSON

The Dishwasher (Local name for the Grey Wagtail)

You flit above the boiling waters, light
on gravel shallow, sarsen stone. Legs flexed
on springs, you knead the foam, life-death to you,
St Vitus jig, your dashing long black tail
and flashing wings. Beneath the waterfall,
your mate's the fan-tailed glider, beard displayed
the tinct of cultured jet, in slow-mo court-
ship flight where you've contrived your sculpted nest.
From kid to youth, no bird's less drab, your cloak
of dark steel-blue, like polished slate against
a perfect northern sky, breast pure citrine,
the scent and hue of the exotic, lure
of artist, poet, vineyard, olive grove,
of lemons grown in dazzling southern light.

PAPER TRAIL   MICHAEL BROWN

It is thought they carried the weight of the world

in the fine-ruled files of their hearts.

We can trace their whereabouts. See for yourself

how our pains taking hours of work

– a labour of love –

have brought us to all but understand

one part of the page of their papery lives.

We have catalogued the till receipts, times,

located the sites, archived the finds.

Now we are just waiting. Waiting

to piece together how it was and why

they left all this behind.

THE SILVER BALLROOM   BRIAN J. BUCHANAN

Against the rules, I am allowed to shuffle around the halls in bare feet. I like the feel of linoleum tile. Now and then a thought stops me; I feel how cold the tiles are unless I stand still long enough to warm them up.

I guess I shuffle because I feel off-balance. I don't want to fall. I worry about falling even though I never fall. I'm told my mind doesn't work right. I guess that's true. It seems to work fine to me, but I can no longer do certain things. I can't put in hours or hold sensible conversations, they say. When I do things, I do them wrong. So they say. Yet I once won a contest for best painting of snow. It was a thickly painted oil of blind lostness, blizzard-blind. No frosty hills or sled tracks or ducks flying south or cabins with chimney smoke.

There's a girl here in restraints, who tries to chomp at everyone with her teeth, big strong teeth. It takes a lot of staff to handle her. Usually I'm not much trouble.

I live among the heavens and the tombs. A great Angel tries to speak through me, but I'm not up to it. I can't translate him to my satisfaction or anyone else's. I think of my bare feet in snow.

When they bring her out of her room, which is seldom, she sits in the hallway. She has to wear the lower half of a goalie mask.

It all just feels like a wide, far wind over a land of roses and graves, when the Angel speaks.

The pills are working, I guess; I don't feel quite as sorrowed as I did. But it feels like there's some muffling force that I must break through but can't break through. I don't like that. Over the tiles I'm trying to get around it.

Irene, my therapist here, had to approve my breaking the rule against bare feet.

Once I tried to translate the Angel in my bare feet in the snow in the middle of the street in Albany.

Irene says I've been talking to her 2x a week for 8 weeks. At first it was 3x a week. I don't understand time, I don't have a sense of it. My mind stops, turns, sometimes I feel nothing, other times too much. My mind is a snow globe.

Irene, Irene. Irene is pretty.

What do you think of me, Irene asked once. I said she reminded me of a white Persian cat. How so? I had to think. Why that? she prompted again. Let me think. Very sleek and confident, elegant. Anything else I remind you of? Yes – you are like a frost-free icebox. She could not hide a little smile. Icebox? An old-fashioned word, isn't it? My parents used that word, I said. The old iceboxes were not frost-free, she said. OK, then a frost-free refrigerator, I said.

We have discussed my parents, both dead now. They were good parents. They didn't understand me. Neither do I. We lived in Portland, Maine.

Sometimes the Angel is dark, immense.

I ask to see the chomping girl. She's very strong, I hear them tell each other. There's something about her eyes – frightened, enraged. Implacable and vulnerable. She's having a hard time right now, the nurses said. Wait till we can bring her out again.

Irene wants me to go into the art room. I don't want to.

My mind feels bruised. Today I trail sorrow across the linoleum tiles. I'm better than I was. Something happened, something broke, something got stripped out of my mind. I stopped functioning correctly, putting in hours. The manager yelled, sat me down in his office, we had a brief talk and he called an ambulance.

Once I had a girlfriend who arranged flowers in a shop in Warsaw, Indiana. Abby had twin dark braids and dark mischievous eyes that would know. When they knew, she left.

Nights are hardest. You cannot break the rules. You're in bed and there's the window.

The moon is a silver ballroom.

Out in the hallway again, the chomping girl glares and growls.

What's your name?

Shh, the nurses say. I'm too loud.

What's your name? I say quietly. She won't answer.

Sonia, the nurses say.

Sonia, you're nice, I say. The Angel said something good about you.

I'm escorted along. Something bitter bit her.

Daytime, after my breakfast and grape juice and pill, I open my window the 6 inches it allows and drink glasses of wind.

Abby, Irene, Sonia. I like their names.

I went in to the florist to see Abby and they said she had left town. Abby had told me she was a nomad and wouldn't stay. Maybe she wasn't really my girlfriend. I am a nomad now too.

We are taken to an art exhibit at a museum. Not Sonia. There's a painting of Mary greeting her older cousin Elizabeth in a small pool of light in great darkness on a stone porch outside a great dark house. Mary and Elizabeth are miraculously pregnant, and greet each other with wonder and joy. The caption says all this. Elizabeth's old husband is hobbling out the door to see, intensely interested. I am overcome. I sit down and sob and then get up and apparently make a disturbance and the outing comes to an end.

Why do they let people like that in here? someone asks as we leave.

Listen to the Angel, I say.

Shh – too loud.

What did the painting mean to you? Irene asks. Everything. How did it make you feel? Too much. Too much what? Too much everything. Anguished happiness. Why? Because I can't get there. Where? To the light on the porch of that great dark house.

It's snowing, the flakes hopping around outside my window. Wild patterns of hopping. No patterns at all. I can feel the snow through the window and the Angel in the hairs on the back of my neck. Maybe the pills aren't working, after all. I take one 2x a day. A siege of sorrow. The silver ballroom has vanished.

I go into the art room and draw lines with wooden sticks on a ball of clay.

Sonia somehow breaks loose and we go on lockdown.

I leave the wooden sticks sticking out of the ball of clay. Automatic metal doors slam in their metal way, echoing. Sonia is injured in the capture and taken away in an ambulance. I raise holy hell. They hold me down for a shot. I can't blame them. I broke something and cut both of my hands on whatever it was.

For a while I don't remember much. When I can think again I discuss matters with the white Persian cat on the frost-free icebox. I ask her out – for sometime when I'm well, I say. She thanks me but says it's not allowed.

If it were allowed, would you? I can't say, she says. Irene, Irene. How are you feeling today? she asks.

I tell her about the structures. Forms, structures, I don't know what to call them. When whatever happened to me happened, my mind was wrecked, it felt like a runaway bus crashed through my fruit stand. My parents were killed in a bus accident so maybe that's why. Except that there was no fruit stand. But my fruit stand was wrecked, all the fruit rolled away down the hill. I look for it. I have been able to build a little rickety table in the art room, I tell Irene. I have been able to build one table and it is because of Sonia and wandering Abby and Mary and Elizabeth, and you, Irene. And now I have broken that table, it feels like.

None of this is what it's really like but it's the best I can do.

I ask to see the chaplain. I didn't know there was one until someone at the nurse's station said the word after I kept going on and on about Mary and Elizabeth. Dave is his name. Reverend Dave. What is wrong with me, Reverend Dave? They don't know, he says, we don't always know. Most of us have things wrong. We must keep on.

How is Sonia?

She will be all right.

I doubt that, she's hurt.

She was hurt, but she'll get better.

I tell him about the Angel. He is very interested. I can't tell him much. The Angel ... I don't know. He's like something far out in the snow that can help me. His calls are indistinct, but I want to hear, so much. Reverend Dave says keep listening. We'll talk some more, whenever I want. He invites me to Sunday services in the chapel. I don't think I could take it. Sometimes people have to be looked after by an orderly so they don't hurt themselves, but they can go. I'd probably be one of those. That's all right, he says.

In the chapel is a painting of a saint. I can just make out broken chains at his feet.

Sonia is back from the hospital and is brought out and sits in the hallway. There's a cast on her arm. In agonised joy I lie prone on my bed, weeping, smiling, laughing, pounding my fists into the mattress. The next day she is out again and I approach her and stand and when the tiles warm up I clasp my hands together before her. She still wears the lower half of a goalie mask. Her eyes are quieter. She watches me.

You are good, I say. I want to take you dancing in the silver ballroom.

I weep and she weeps. The nurses cluster around because she has said her first words since she has been here: Thank you.

It's a few weeks till Christmas. Out my window I watch ducks in Santa hats, singing in the snow on Lake Ontario.

Don't ducks fly south for the winter? Irene asks.

Not these ducks.

ORDERING THE WEDDING SAREE   JO BURNS

Weaver, weave me a crimson poem,
set your pattern, follow my form,
metre by metre, fresco me a prayer,
a *Puja* offering of fuchsia, gold

brocade, jacquard and scarlet warp,
burnt orange weft through vermillion
silk, as roseate as Tagore's sun
kissed jasmine, lotus, bougainvillea,

frangipani, King's mantle, periwinkle,
as terracotta gives hyacinth, hibiscus.
Make me Parvati, love's docile goddess.
Make me Mohini, make my groom Shiva.

Make me Sita, a woman like no other.
Make me the Shakti of both wealth and wisdom.
Weave me Vedas, stitch my future
in canna lily, rosella, tulis.

Make me a deity for my Rama,
in my saree from a Kancheepuram loom.
Weaver, make me the crimson poem.
Set your pattern, follow my given form.

CASTLES IN SPAIN   SANDRA BUNTING

For Eleanor and Willy

One moment you are dancing in rain:
waves sing a love song, winds twirl you,

vast skies change moods for you under
the benevolent influence of a soft day

a damp-wool smell of comfort:
you have a life and someone to love.

Then suddenly the shudder of clouds
crushes you under its weight like pounding

sea on coastal rocks, no hint of mercy;
home changes to a grey prison, a dead end.

*

With help, your water-saturated soul
is plucked up and flown to the south

dropped among the mountains of Spain
where sun coaxes back crumbly life,

You explore castles of long ago
burnt solid into dry cracked earth,

perky fountains concealed in courtyards
lush flowers, fragrance of lemon.

*

And so you can go home again,
strength, like a vine, props you up,

lets you return to a wild river, stormy
stone fences, daffodils against a wall.

You're, once again, exhilarated by wind,
walk refreshed in constant downpour,

past fiddlers in the pub, a sense of place
lost for a moment, now filling the void.

LISTENING FOR CODE   EDEL BURKE

I attune to the tap of a hammer
fixing felt to next door's garden shed,
before rapid bursts distract me.
I remember last year, that same noise
untraced and afterwards I found

a worn-out starling on the attic floor.
I climbed up, conscious
of the rhythm of my own beat.
Then the bird appears, stands in a flush
thrown in by the skylight.

She pulses with fear,
flits and flaps her pointed wings, flies
to where light disperses more evenly,
then points her beak to the glass and
returns, repeats, as if to show me.

I crawl up, lean to the window, open it,
she follows, sits for a moment,
sets her brown speckled frame outward
bound, her metallic green sheen pours
the length of her and she's gone.

In two days we are back there, in our own
rooftop roost, bruised and breathless.
I resolve to permanent sealing, until she eyes
me a cornered look and I imagine the
blue polished shells and repent.

DECEPTIVE SAND DUNES   ALI ZNAIDI

after Jeremy Schmidt's Action-Adventure (After Wyatt)

I pack all the corroded clouds and plenty
of whispers and head to the desert.

A road I haven't taken since a decade
or so. The desert is no longer soft
because more and more thorns adorn the dunes.

Even the cacti's prickles become thicker,
despite the drought.

Even the poisons of snakes drop in false nonchalance
(in the form of soap bubbles wanting to reach the sky).

The sun (intoxicated with its Dadaist glow) no longer
bestows its lights on the sand.

There's nothing but deception.
There's nothing but deceptive sand dunes.
There's nothing but barren clouds.
There's nothing but the corroded clouds.
Plenty of (barren) whispers and those I have already packed
also abound – this is what I call
a harbinger of an unbearable tragedy.

WHITE DREAMS   COLETTE COEN

The water is tepid. The white bubbles that promised cleanliness disappear after the first dunk of the cloth. There are so many cupboards. Too many for a one bedroom flat, as though some crazed workman thought that she would have the money to fill them. Jess had lifted out the tins while she boiled the kettle for water (she's not meant to do that), and they sit there, showing her menu for the rest of the week. Tomato soup for Wednesday; beans on toast – Thursday; tuna and sweet corn, their fish for Friday. Saturday she'd have to go to the shops again.

She squeezes the J cloth, a fresh one every Tuesday, feels the nip of detergent in her cracked fingers and starts to wipe. On tiptoes she stretches right into the back corner where there are always crumbs, although she doesn't know how they get there. Then the mottled cream sides, the doors, front and back, the underside of the cupboard, the roof of it.

She chucks out the water, pours some more, splashing in bleach for the tiles, looks at her hands, wrinkled like an old woman's. Chloe's little cough speckles through the wall, but Jess thinks she'll settle – hopes she will. She moves the breadbin, cleans behind it, praying that by the time Chloe grows up she'll have a garden to play in.

The chamois she bought from the boy at the door begins to disintegrate as she rubs it over the window. She looks out to the city, to the back end of the supermarket, to the woman in the red t-shirt who runs by at the same time every Tuesday. For a moment she lets her mind wander, trying to imagine a life where she would have the time to jog. Mind you, she ran all the time – for the bus, to the shops.

If she scrubs the uPVC the stains might come off, but the yellowed frames will never be white again. A smoker must have been here before her, or maybe that's just what time does, like it does to your face.

Chloe's still restless and Jess wonders if she'll be able to make the bed without disturbing her. Monday's meant to be the night she does that, but the sheets had taken longer to dry because she didn't have any money for her card until today, and she had to let them dry by the window rather than on the heater. (She's not meant to do that either.) At least it had been a nice day, and she could have the window wide, and get Chloe out for a walk round the centre. Her cough has got a little better, but Doctor England said that the puffers will take a while before they really start to work. He's written another report, changed her medication too, but doesn't think it will make much of a difference.

Wednesdays she doesn't clean, she just gives the surfaces and cupboards a quick wipe, and then the bathroom tiles, and the cistern of course. She goes out with her sister, leaves her mum to wash the dishes – first the ones they've used for their tea, then the ones from the cupboard, there's not much – just the set Auntie Fran gave her when she moved in, and a couple of big plates she bought at the car boot sale a few weeks ago. It would be lovely to get to use them one day, plonk a roast on them for Sunday dinner. Her mum isn't as thorough with the washing these days, with her arthritis and whatnot, so sometimes if she has time before her shift, she'll rinse them again on Friday, just to make sure.

At the weekend she does the real work. With Chloe at Jamie's mum's she can attack the toys and crib. Washing everything first with Fairy (her mum was horrified when she bought the stuff from the pound shop, said she might as well not bother), then the sterilising solution from the chemist. She has nightmares about the germs that might be lurking on the toys. She tried for weeks to stop Chloe from putting them in her mouth, but she couldn't watch her every hour of the day, not with so much to do, so she just has to make sure they're as clean as they can be. The soft toys she throws in the washing machine with the pink baby-gros when she does the laundry. She doesn't think the toys will last, not the way her Baby Annabell did. Right the way through childhood looking as bright and clean as she had on Christmas morning, until she came here. Then one day she looked and realised Annabell couldn't stay. It was sad that she couldn't even pass her on, give her to Patsy for her little one, or even hand her in to Oxfam, since they were so good to her. But Annabell was too filthy. She couldn't bear the thought that she might infect someone else.

She doesn't know if Jamie even sees Chloe anymore, she's afraid to ask his mum, not sure what she wants the answer to be. He didn't understand Jess – called her a fucking lunatic, psycho bitch. Not when they met, of course, when he was trying to get inside her knickers. No, it was only once she was pregnant and they'd got the flat together that he started all the just leave my mug there for Christ's sake, I might want another brew. She couldn't leave it there, no matter how hard she tried. She had a system, a routine handed down through three generations in the high-rise. Don't leave liquid lying around – down the sink, rinse, mug away. She thought he was beginning to understand when he bought her a MagiMop for her birthday, but then she heard him with Dean, get her a French maid's outfit if she likes dusting so much, get her to fluff you up. She stopped her daily wipe of the back of his wardrobe after that, let the white spots eat into his kit making him smell like an old man.

Water slops from the bucket over the floor. She'll need to get a new mop head when she's out again, and more bleach, and cream cleaner.

She looks at the clock on the wall – she'll need to clean it tomorrow. The black spores are forming again, working their way around the face, giving her an alternative view of time, of days. She'll make a cup of tea. Leave footprints on the clean floor. Boil the kettle and steam up the kitchen. Whenever she goes to the Council, or her MP, or MSP, they tell her the same thing. You can't dry your washing inside. You have to keep steam to a minimum. The black spores are only condensation marks. Any links to pulmonary problems are purely coincidental. You just need to keep the place clean.

The clock stutters to eight o'clock, so she takes her tea to bed, the only place to keep warm, flicks through a magazine showing pictures of cupcakes and retro aprons, and drifts off to sleep. She sleeps soundly, dreaming white dreams.

ADVENT SONG   PATRICK DEVANEY

for Nya, born on the winter solstice

You arrive at a period of doubt,
the established order giving way
to discord and building of fences,
refugees overcrowding frail vessels,
nuclear missiles being readied,
rivers polluted, icecaps receding,
wildlife-rich jungles cut down.

You look at us adults wide-eyed,
seemingly attempting to grasp
why your former idyll's been swapped
for this bleak arena you've entered
like a snowdrop in frost-chilled ground
or the solstice's first ray of sunshine
flooding a burial mound.

BUT STILL IT MOVES   PATRICK DEELEY

But still it moves is a phrase attributed by some to Galileo in 1633 when forced by the
Roman Church to recant his claims that the Earth moves around the Sun, rather than the
converse.

It moves, Galileo – the world, the universe, the billions
on billions of miles of observational space
still expanding, Edward Hubble says, and still we imagine
we are the life and soul, the one sentient hub
of the place. Still we look up, look anew – of a day
to read the weather, of a night to lose ourselves
in the hush that comes over us, call it wonderment
waiting to be met. A giant tortoise serving as a griddle
for the flat plate of the earth – not even as children
did we fancy there was that. But Ptolemy
we could picture – in our gripping of stars and planets
each to its approved spot on classroom walls
with blue-tack, or in the hoodwink of the heavens
as undeviating, before we learned how Copernicus had run
those circles in orderly courses about the sun.
You, then, never allowed out again because you dared
to let unwanted truths in; still Jupiter juggles
its moons just as you saw them, still the dance continues
after you've gone; after Newton's apple
hasn't clocked him on the head but 'occasion'd'
his notions about gravity; after Einstein has theorised
on what 'speed' can mean and 'spacetime' do;
after Hawking and co envisage tying together the job lot,
huge with miniscule, while stirring string theory
into the cosmological pot. Meanwhile, for me, this night
waits to be taken to bed. Maybe I'll dream
the twelve-ton 'Leviathan of Parsonstown' I saw today,

whose cooped pine boards – painted black –
set me thinking of a barrel to beat all barrels, our island's
once-upon-a-time world's biggest telescope,
the way it bulges at the middle as though it's gulped a deep
draught of space; dream the heavens as they shift
through its original speculum-metal eye
and how the faraway look we feel we inherit or are given to
holds us fervent, tranquil while the weight
of the world and its troubles in our watching seems to lift.

STILL LIFE WITH RED ROSES AND BUTCHY
TRICIA DEARBORN

After Max Beckmann, *Stillben mit Roten Rosen und Butchy*, 1942 (oil on canvas)

The painter promised her
marriage, and a fresh bouquet
each day. She just had to lay down

her bow, stop singing; forgo
all thought of children.
She'd have the little dog

to dote on. And the roses.
When she leans to sniff them
their velvet fleshiness, the slight

waxy drag against her lips,
is like the vernixed skin
of newborns she will neither

smell nor hold. Sometimes
she plucks a single petal, grinds it
between her fingertips.

The clear red juice, dark strings
of flesh, are like the harbingers
of barren cramp.

Even when that monthly taunt
has ceased
his roses will bloom daily.

Each day she takes up scissors
to snip woody stalks, arrange again
the twelve small heads.

WHAT YOU WANT, WHAT YOU NEED, WHAT YOU GET
JESSE FALZOI

He immediately recognizes her voice. It's me, she says, and he says, Hi, Lydia, and then she says, You have a son. Do you want to see him?

A son? he says.

Lydia suggests next Sunday. If that's okay with you.

He wants to ask her why she didn't get in touch before, but all he says is, Sunday's fine.

There's a photograph he took of her when they were on the Baltic coast: she is squinting against the sun, waving at him. He puts it against the pile of books on his night stand. She seems too young to become a mother.

The next morning he has breakfast at the café around the corner. A man holding a sleeping baby is sitting at the next table, reading a magazine. From time to time the man caresses its head. Then, suddenly, there is this woman with unkempt hair. She kisses the man on the mouth. They talk and they laugh, and, every other minute, they yawn as if they have just come home from a party. She takes the baby and puts it to her breast. It sucks and sucks and eventually looks to the side, exposing the nipple and a drop of milk running down the breast.

He tells his boss that he's got the flu. He buys his first pack of cigarettes after four years as a non-smoker. He drinks two bottles of Rioja a day. Her picture on the nightstand; he gently touches her belly, tries to visualize it growing.

One night they sat on a bench next to the TV tower. They shared a bottle of cheap wine and took off their clothes and jumped into the basins. They picked roses from the bushes and threw them into the night. At dawn he carried her back to the bench and she put her head on his lap and he carefully removed the petals from her wet hair.

After six days he gets up to take a shower and a shave. He arrives at the station much too early. Perhaps they won't come, he tells himself. He walks along the platform until the train approaches. She gets off, wearing a summer dress and high heels. He only remembers jeans and sneakers. And the leather jacket with the 'Enola Gay' patch. Hello, she says, stretching out her hand that he barely dares to touch.

His son is tall. He looks like the guy from the student card he found on the bottom of the photo box. Except for the eyes, which are blue like the mid-morning Sardinian sea.

Lydia says, This is Finn.

Hello, his son says with a strikingly deep voice, hands buried in the pockets of his sweatpants.

I'll go for a walk, okay? She bites her lower lip. Seventeen years ago, she said, What do you want from me? and he said, What do you mean? and she bit her lower lip and he went to the kitchen to get another bottle of beer.

He clears his throat and looks at his son. You're hungry?

On the escalator he notices that his son's army bag is unzipped. You shouldn't do that, he says.

His son frowns.

There's a lot of pickpocketing around here. He stops in front of a Burger King. What about here?

I'm vegetarian.

They got fish.

His son raises the eyebrows. There's a scar above the right one.

He points at a bakery. A sandwich?

They leave the station with two cheese sandwiches. Have you been here before? he asks.

Sure, his son says.

Often?

Couple of times.

He sits down on a bench. His son moves away from him as far as possible, bending over his ludicrously large Nikes.

And, he says, do you like it?

His son removes the lettuce from the sandwich and throws it onto the lawn. It's

35

all right.

Looking at his son's shoddy sweatpants, he says, You're still at school? He doesn't get more than a nod, but he goes on, And? He takes his son's shrugging for a sign that it could be better. Got plans for your future?

No.

He notices the long dirty fingernails of the right hand. The left hand hardly had any. Play the guitar?

Yeah.

Lydia sometimes joined him when he was practising with his band. She sat next to the amp, reading a book. Once, he asked her to sing. She hesitated, then stood up, then took the microphone. Her voice was strange and beautiful. He looks at his son. He tries to picture Lydia singing him to sleep when he was little. You have a band?

No. His son stuffs the last part of his sandwich into his mouth, rummages in his bag, produces a small metal box.

He imagines Lydia telling his son that his father played the guitar too. He imagines Lydia thinking of him when they went to a shop to buy the first guitar. I used to play, too.

His son nods, turning the box around in his hands.

He clears his throat and says, What kind of music do you like?

All kinds, his son says.

Come on, he says, which bands do you like?

His son takes a hand-rolled cigarette out of the box, lights it, takes a deep drag. The Stones, AC/DC.

He sniffs. You better put that out.

His son leans back, grinning. This is Berlin, right?

What about your mother?

She's fine with it, his son says. As long as I stick to the rule.

What rule?

His son takes a pair of sunglasses out of his bag and puts them on. Only weekends and holidays.

Then he often smoked pot. Lydia sometimes took one or two drags. Once, at a party in Kreuzberg, she smoked more than the usual and vanished after a while. Weeks later somebody told him that she had collapsed on the bathroom floor and that the paramedics had to be called. He looks around, wondering if she is watching. Your mother and I went to the gig at Waldbühne.

What gig?

Thunderstruck was the first song, he says. Fucking brilliant.

His son lets out the smoke through his nose, and says, O-kay.

He still has her mix tape. On the cover there is a collage of band photos, inside the titles in her neat handwriting. She must have spent hours with that tape and he only listened to it once or twice. When he wanted to listen to it last night, his tape deck wasn't working anymore.

A boy wearing a Bulls cap sits down on the next bench, dragging a girl onto his lap. She whispers something into his ear.

He says, winking, Your mum still looks great.

His son reaches into the pocket of his sweatpants, takes out a smartphone, starts writing.

Got a girlfriend?

Happiness is being single.

The speakers announce a regional train to Stralsund. That's where he took Lydia's picture. The condom ripped on the second night. She told him not to worry, so he didn't. I had no idea, he says, I would have taken care of you.

Eyes fixed on the display of his cell, his son says, No sweat.

He even helped her move. He helped her carry her stuff downstairs, drove the rented van to Hannover, helped her carry her stuff up to the top floor. He went to the balcony to smoke a cigarette and promised to visit soon. Then he drove the van back to Berlin. The two hundred mark deposit had been lying in his drawer for six months, before he finally managed to send it to her by registered mail.

His son finishes the water bottle and burps. Gotta go, he says.

He puts a hand on his son's shoulder. Give us a chance.

Why?

Cause you gotta know your father, he says. And I gotta know my son.

You can't always get what you want. His son lifts his sunglasses. That's what Carsten would say.

Who's Carsten?

Her boyfriend.

You forgot something.

His son's eyes. The colour of the Sardinian sea. His lips hardly opening when he says, Did I?

If you try sometime?

His son puts his sunglasses back on. Whatever.

Coming back to the station he realizes that Lydia has been watching them the whole time. She gets up from the bench and says, There you are.

There we are, he says.

To his surprise their son is able to smile. You're all right, mom?

Lydia says, Did he behave? She checks her watch although there is a huge clock on the wall. Thank you for coming.

He smiles. What are your plans for tomorrow? He looks at their son, then at Lydia, then says, Can I invite you for dinner?

I'll call you, Lydia says.

She seemed so sure when she told him that she would continue her studies in Hannover. He didn't dare ask for the reason. He clears his throat, and then says, We could have rocked the thing together.

Lydia says, What do you mean?

Let's go, mum, his son says.

She extends her hand. He takes it, holds on to it, pulls her close. He puts his arms around her. Out of reflex probably, she embraces him. He feels her breathe out. He feels her relax.

And when his son tries to pull them apart, he turns around and takes him into his arms too.

FORGIVENESS CEREMONY   JESSAMINE O CONNOR

Having watched the forgiveness ceremony at Standing Rock

I want to kneel down into these reeds, feel bogwater
creep around my knees, sink
my hands deep, bow –
to the low sun, the small trees,
beg forgiveness
for my car, my stove,
my electrified house.

I need to put my face in the ground
and almost – but not quite –
drown in the land
to plead mercy
for my laziness, my apathy,
my fattening lack of passion
and all the excuses I will ever make.

KILMACURRA

for Kaeden

One day when the world
was smoky with October
we left the path behind, climbing
into the dark of oak and yew. I craved
the magic that the path forbids, wanted
to show you that even beyond
what hands create and feet wear thin
there is a holiness that trickles like a spring
through this broken world.
That bravery is sometimes in the leaving of the path,
in the seeing;
that it is impossible to ignore the grace of it,
the cold that takes over, the sunspots
between the trees, breathing warmth
into a dying landscape.

I watched the squirrel, grey fur turned up
against the wind, claws and paws seeking yield,
eyes pooling around the sleep of seasons.
And still you slept on,
skin all newness and pale, welcoming the chill,
the air, the sun warming
making what was once untouched
ruddy with the stroke of autumn.
Your hands grasped in tiny paws, breath
as steady as the gathering of harvest –
predictable, crucial,
it was everything.

And then the squirrel climbed higher
to view what was left. She paced the branch
worrying a path, steady in her concern.
And your eyes opened to the dapples of sun,
the soft patter of clawed feet above,
the same blue
that holds up the sky.

SCARECROW SINGS THE HIGH LONESOME
ROBERT OKAJI

Nothing about me shines or sparkles. If asked,
I would place myself among the discarded –
remnant cloth and straw, worn, inedible,
useless, if not for packaging intended to
convey a certain message, which I of course
have subverted to 'Welcome, corvids!' Even
my voice lies stranded in the refuse, silent
yet harmonious, clear yet strangled, whole
and unheard, dispersed, like tiny drops of
vapour listing above the ocean's swell, enduring
grey skies and gulls and those solemn rocks
bearing their weight against the white crush.
Why do I persist? What tethers a shadow
to its body? How do we hear by implication
what isn't there? Bill Monroe hammered
his mandolin, chopping chords, muting,
droning, banging out incomplete minors
to expectant ears, constructing more than
a ladder of notes climbing past the rafters
into the smoky sky. What I sing is not
heard but implied: the high lonesome, blue
and old-time, repealed. Crushed limestone
underfoot. Stolen names, borrowed sounds.
Dark words subsumed by light, yellowed,
whitened, faded to obscurity, to obscenity.

DEATH'S CHILD   TANYA FARRELLY

'Bernard, stay still. Don't worry about what's over my shoulder.' Treasa, the social club coordinator, leaned in, her red lips and white face no more than an inch from his as she pencilled a black line round his eyes and then smudged it with her fingertips. Her nails glinted metallic silver. 'Such long lashes,' she said, fingering them as he blinked, 'any girl would die for those.' She straightened and Bernie allowed his eyes to refocus. Treasa stood before him, long legs covered only by a man's white t-shirt, a red sticky substance running down its front. Her dark hair was back-combed, riotous. She kept brushing it back from her huge blue eyes. 'Shame you didn't dress up,' she said. 'You'd have made a mean Vampire Le Stat.' She dipped her finger in the red paint and trailed a sliver of blood down his right cheek.

There was more excitement among the staff than the students, Bernie reckoned. The staffroom had become home to zombies, and several sexy witches who milled round in tight black dresses sporting pointy hats or devil horns. If they strolled through Temple Bar they could almost be mistaken for a hen party. 'Treasa, what are you supposed to be?' one of the witches shouted across the room. Treasa shrugged. 'Death's Child,' she said. 'More creative than a trying-to-be-sexy witch anyway,' she mumbled, giving Bernie a wink. 'Right, you're done Bern,' she said. 'Who's next?'

In the bar, Bernie was almost sorry he hadn't worn a costume, he felt more obvious because he looked normal. Normal was the kind of thing to attract attention on a night like this. The room was thronging with students. He saw Alvaro from Madrid flirting with Cynthia from Sao Paolo who was wearing – if wearing was not too strong a verb – a Wonder Woman costume that left little to wonder about.

The teachers, all bar Seanie who was mingling with the students, were clustered in a corner of the room. Bernie tuned in and out of the conversation and watched Seanie laughing with a girl in a Little Red Riding Hood costume. As though they sensed his eyes on them, they both suddenly turned. Seanie raised his beer glass to Bernie and gestured for him to join them. Embarrassed, Bernie saw no alternative and made his way through the tightly woven group between him and his friend.

Seanie. You'd think he'd have learned his lesson after the last time, but no – the students were adults, as he put it, and that meant fair game. Bernie liked Seanie, but sometimes he couldn't believe the nerve of the man. He'd marched into the director's office and asked her to move a student from his class after he'd had a one-night thing with her. He'd been a gentleman, he'd said, even dropped her back into the city centre the next morning, but the girl had expected more – a relationship maybe. She'd started undermining him in class, making pointed comments. He figured she'd told some of the other students too. He'd had to tell the DOS what happened and the girl had been moved, without so much as a reprimand for Seanie, to another class.

'Teacher!' Bernie was waylaid by a hand on his arm on his way to the men's. He turned to see Alessandro and Victor. The two boys were never apart. Neither had shown up for class that week. 'Where have you two been?' Bernie asked them. Victor laughed. 'Sorry, teacher. We had parties all weekend.'

'Weekend?' Bernie said. 'But this is Wednesday!'

'It was a long weekend,' Victor grinned.

Alessandro nudged Bernie. 'What you think of the Brazilian girls, teacher? Hot, yeah?' He mimicked a burning movement with his hand and laughed.

Bernie laughed in turn, but didn't comment. He saw Seanie and Little Red Riding Hood disappear, probably gone out for a smoke. He exchanged a bit of banter with the two boys before disengaging himself and heading for the toilet.

He was climbing the stairs when he heard a sound, a laugh. Feet silent on the thick red carpet, Bernie stopped at the turn of the stairs to listen, then stole quietly towards the sound. A door was open just off the corridor. He noticed that there was no handle on the outside. He pushed the door open a couple of inches. It was a store room of some kind, and enough light shone from the streetlight outside for Bernie to make out two figures standing opposite the window. Seanie? A flash of white, a moan – jingle of steel as a belt was undone. No! Bernie stepped back. A foreign voice whispering 'baby' as the hands crept beneath Death's Child's t-shirt. Bernie made her out in the orange haze – hair askew, bare legs wrapped round the waist of a cowboy as he slammed her hard against the wall.

'Christ,' Bernie thought. Treasa. And her with a long-term boyfriend. A nice guy, who normally showed up at the staff nights out. Conor, was that his name? He'd seen him tagged in Treasa's Facebook pictures. What the hell was the girl thinking? Silently, Bernie withdrew. He went into the men's and locked himself in a cubicle, ashamed that the sight of Treasa had got him aroused. Pretty, quirky Treasa. He'd have tried it himself if he'd thought he'd stood a chance. But not when she had a boyfriend, there were lines you just didn't cross. Anger surfaced as he remembered what a fool Deirdre had made of him. Six months it had been going on, she'd looked him full in the face and admitted it, no more remorse than a sociopath. She'd got bored, she said. Bored, that was a laugh and she the one who sat at home day after day watching mindless television series. He didn't think she'd the energy to actually cheat on him.

Bernie cast a look at the door of the storeroom before hurrying down the stairs. He didn't hear anything. He practically collided with the school director as he pushed open the door to the bar. 'Bernie,' she said. 'She got you, too.' 'What?' The director waved her hand, 'Treasa, she did a great job on the faces.' Bernie didn't answer. He was taken aback for a moment by the director's outfit; a small black bowler was perched over her slick black bob. She'd glued fake lashes on one eye and a set of braces covered her man's white shirt. 'Barbara,' Bernie started. The eye was disconcerting. 'Not tonight, Bernie. Tonight, I'm Alex,' she said. Bernie tried to smile, he had one eye on the door waiting for Treasa and the cowboy to return. He leaned in towards the director. 'Maybe this is none of my business,' he said, 'but what if I were to tell you I'd seen a member of staff with a student upstairs? I know there's no rule against it per se, but ...' Barbara moved closer. He smelt wine on her breath when she whispered, 'Where?' 'There's a storeroom. Turn right when you get to the top of the stairs.' Bernie went to get his coat. When he looked round the room, the director was gone. He stopped to talk to a couple of teachers on the way out, huddled outside the door, smoking. 'Have you seen Seanie?' he asked them. They shook their heads. He'd expected to find him sharing a cigarette with Little Red Riding Hood.

It was quiet in the staffroom the next morning. Two of the teachers had phoned in sick and the director was hopping. Bernie glanced into the office on his way to class, but Treasa's desk was empty. He wondered if she'd rung in, too sick and ashamed to turn up for work or if the director had got to her. If she'd come upon her in the storeroom with her cowboy.

At break time, the director stuck her head out of the office and called him. He went in, heart skipping, wondering if she were about to tell him what had happened with Treasa. 'Bernie, is there any chance you could cover a class this afternoon?' she asked. Bernie considered for a minute. 'Yeah, sure. What level is it?' 'Upper-int. You should find the notes in Sean's folder.' Barbara didn't look up and Bernie left the office feeling almost dissed. She was in some mood today. It seemed the staff weren't the only ones hungover.

'Where's Sean?' one of the students asked. 'I don't know,' Bernie said. 'Sick, I think.' The blonde girl who Bernie recognised as Little Red Riding Hood looked concerned. He wondered if she'd spent the night with him.

Bernie was surprised when he finished class to see Seanie in the director's office. He moved around the staff room, pretending not to look, but everyone could see through the plate glass that separated the office from the staff room. The director was sitting erect in her leather chair, Seanie slumped somewhat in front of her. Bernie saw him spread his hands in a 'what can I say?' gesture. The director stood and Seanie did too. He didn't look happy. Bernie looked down at his papers as the door opened. He felt Seanie stop and pick up his coat from a chair nearby. He looked up. 'Seanie, I took your class this afternoon. I've written it up for you.' Bernie waved the folder at Seanie. The director came out of her office walking quickly, head down. She looked upset. Seanie looked after her. 'Don't worry about it, Bern,' he said. He pulled on his leather jacket. 'Be seeing you,' he said. A few people looked up and mumbled goodbye.

Friday came and Seanie hadn't returned. Bernie bumped into Treasa at the photocopier. She smiled at him – her red-coated smile. Her bracelets jingled as she worked the machine. 'How's Conor these days?' Bernie asked her. The smile left Treasa's face. 'Ah, I couldn't tell you, Bern. We're not together anymore.' 'Oh God, I'm sorry.' Bern touched her braceleted arm. 'It's okay, we split up about three months ago.' 'Ah, okay. Sure, maybe we could get a coffee sometime. If you want to talk or anything.' He hoped it sounded casual. Treasa smiled. 'Yeah, maybe,' she said. She glanced round the room and then leaned in conspiratorially. 'Have you heard about Seanie?' she said. Bernie shook his head. 'He's not coming back. Apparently, the director walked in on him the other night with a student.' Bernie made a surprised sound. 'Not against the rules though, is it?' he said. Treasa raised an arched eyebrow and gathered her papers. 'Not yet, but they'll get you on something else. Think from here on in we'll all have to be careful.'

His eyes followed the sway of Treasa's hips as she climbed the stairs. Poor Seanie, he'd wondered where he'd vanished to with Little Red Riding Hood.

DECEMBER IN KILLASPUGLONANE   KNUTE SKINNER

One of the pleasures of December
in Killaspuglonane
is the twisted calligraphy
of our bare thorn tree.

Another is the view we have,
in between its branches,
of a high green meadow glazed
by the winter sun.

THE BALLAD OF TULLYKYNE   NICOLA GEDDES

King is to castle as tower is to rook
My sister's fort is as tall as mine
The rain it battered and the wind it shook
She watches me from behind her line
Her eyes hard and wary, she stares out alone
Cold creeping into each cranny and nook
She thinks she is safe in her fortress of stone
King is to castle as tower is to rook

High is the tower and cold is the brook
At a table for one she is served up her wine
The cup to her lips like an old fish hook
On touching her tongue the drink sours to brine
And cursing and spitting she clutches her throne
Her face is reset in that pinched, crooked look
As old and as cracked as the grey limestone
King is to castle as tower is to rook

My sister the witch! My sister the crook!
I call up her ruin, and wait for the sign
I cast down three stones and forward I look
To the fall of the fortress of old Tullykyne
But the storm that crashed down, and the wind that was blown
The strength of the lightning, oh how I mistook!
The cry of defeat was both hers and my own
King is to castle as tower is to rook

Raven and crow, jackdaw and rook
A young man came by in black feathers so fine
In his right hand a knife, in his left was a book
He fashioned figures from my sister's spine

A miniature horse from my collarbone
He wound our hair round his button hook
Before setting the pieces on the square cornerstone
King is to castle as tower is to rook

Our deeds are forgotten, our names are unknown
The crows all gather on the ruin by the brook
The gorse, the fuchsia and the hawthorn have grown
King is to castle as tower is to rook.

LAVENDER ROAD   MADELAINE NERSON MAC NAMARA

We're introduced. I climb behind.
My arms knot tight around your waist.
Two motorbikes, the speed of wind
upon the skin,
a straight tree-lined lavender road
thrill and terror.
Friend of my friend's friend I'll never
meet you again.

For twice an hour your belly's warmth
my only grip onto this world.
With, in between, the sun above
the cherry tree, this June picnic
our chins that run with red black juice.
And I pretend this will go on
until I die and know it won't
and know it will.

THE BONE THAT CRACKS THE LOUDEST   SEAN GILL

A rat breeds a little faster, lives a little harder, and dies a little uglier than any man. Usually it is a cruel death, a flurry of claw and teeth, the will to live snapped off at the hilt. Few rats go gentle into that good night, and consequently, the world of the rat is clogged rotten with ghosts in ways men can scarcely understand.

A wandering rat must exercise caution when passing by a laboratory; that foul earth is roamed by phantom battalions who met their end in gruesome experiments. It is common for these ghosts to press down upon the living en masse, depriving their victim of the ability to flee. It isn't long before some predator snatches the life from the unfortunate, paralyzed soul.

A poisoned rat leaves behind a bitter wraith; a false whisper on the wind, spreading harmful rumours. Travellers may have the sudden urge to eat tainted meat, carelessly roam toxic wastes, or turn a blind eye to fresh sustenance.

The ghosts of rats who have died in glue traps sing the song of the sirens, an irresistible call that prompts a shared fate, the victims' paws sinking softly into the hell of the glue, a long and sorry withering away.

A spring-loaded trap results in fewer ghosts because it kills so unexpectedly, but that is not to say I have never seen such a spirit, lurching along with a crushed spine and a twisted neck, dragging his dead half behind him. They say that misery loves company, but in the span of an eternity, misery can learn to love misery.

A drowning rat can tread for eighty hours straight before he succumbs to a watery grave. Therefore, the ghosts of drowned rats are the most tenacious, seizing wayward tails in iron grips and dragging their victims down, down, down.

Finally, there are the ghosts of rats who have died in blood sport. I have heard it said that, captive and helpless, anticipating the hound, their souls curdle before they die, leaving twisted apparitions who writhe like speared eels, screaming in agony, coated in slobber and blood, unable to commune with the living or the dead. This is untrue. I can speak with authority on this subject, for I am one of them.

*

I lived in a sewer, but there were worse places to call home. Now and forever I live

51

in the pit, occupying simultaneously three moments in time.

The first is when I am poured from the squirming sack. Along with ninety-nine of my comrades, I am rotating, nearly frozen, in mid-air. I catch my first glimpse of the pit: no more than three yards square, a patch of earth surrounded by splintery barricades. Atop the barricades is a thin moat of burning oil, illuminating the space and casting lank shadows. In the centre of the pit is Bucky, an Airedale Terrier, a hound of monstrous size coated in thickets of shaggy brown hair. His whiskers hang low on his chops, concealing his fangs. Such dogs have been trained from birth to hunt little furry things, snatch them in their jaws, and shake them unto death. Bucky is known for his achievements in this field; he has once killed a hundred rats in six minutes and fourteen seconds. Tonight he intends to outdo himself.

Beyond the pit and the flame is a steep tunnel of human faces, shoulder to shoulder, spiralling upward unto infinity. By firelight, the faces are identical, stiffly framed by waxed moustaches and capped with stovepipe hats. They look down on this slop sink of mortality and cast a shroud of judgment. Warmed by the flames, it condenses into a thin mist, then recedes.

Adrift, with the tunnel above and the jaws below, I cry out for balance. In life, it was a half-second before we ploughed into the dirt and swarmed the four corners of the pit, striving in vain to climb the walls. In death, I reside in that moment, a statue suspended above a waiting tomb.

*

The second is when the light is extinguished. A lake of glowing blood wells in the dirt. Bucky has slain four dozen of my friends, each death proclaimed by a snap of fluid and crack of bone. I hear it still, echoing as a single tone, thicker and louder than it was in life, penetrating and all-encompassing. One moment I'm scraping at the wall with empty claws, and in the next I'm between Bucky's jaws, only his grip isn't so true – he has me by the hindquarter, not the torso – and I have room to lunge, lashing out with my teeth. I dive into the jelly of his eye, and it bursts wet on my lips. At this, the gathered crowd gasps in unison, outraged, and the air in the room is sucked up through the tunnel and into their lungs. Deprived of oxygen, the moat of flame twitches, shudders, and suffocates. At once the pit is as dark and wet as a sewer pipe. I occupy this moment also: dangling, impaled, the remnants of the hound's eye caked fresh across my snout, witness to a coiling mass of rage and disgust, their gaping mouths entrenched suddenly by darkness.

*

The third is when the room implodes. Bucky releases and flings me against the wall. An odour of fear flows down from the tunnel and drips into the pit. There is an awful clamour as the men battle one another to escape, tripping over chairs and groping at shadows, and then they too begin to fall, stumbling over the edges of the steep drop. Though dying, in the black I see with sound and smell, and it is the men who have lost their bearings now, landing crooked on broken necks, their stovepipe hats fluttering after them.

*

In the layers of this triptych I attract and I repel; I dwell on a bubble of force, a deepening twilight, a cosmic abstraction. The world shrinks and the world expands. We have no desires, no aspirations, no encumbrances. The living prefer to imagine vengeful spirits, as if to justify their own shortcomings. In seeking to understand our silence, they say it must be immortal agony that keeps us from our haunting. This is untrue. It is indifference.

CIRCUMCISION PARTY   TERESA GODFREY

In the eastern Mediterranean when darkness falls, it falls suddenly as if a cloth of navy silk, embroidered with white stars, has been thrown over the whole world. Away from the tourist areas, pools of dull, yellow light from street lamps, cafes and huckster shops dapple the narrow back streets. Huge television sets blaze through open doorways and cast flickering shadows across vine-draped verandas.

The veranda of the biggest house – the one on the corner – is full of women preparing chillies. The younger ones are bareheaded while the older women wear scarves loosely tied under their jutting chins. There is a long, low couch against the back wall and various stools and boxes have been borrowed from within to provide seating for them all. They form a circle around the mound of chillies and murmur in tones as warm and full as the night air. Occasionally one breaks into a peal of laughter and they all laugh as if something has released itself inside them. Then they forget to murmur for a while and chatter loudly until they remember again while, inside the house, the men stare at pale, western actors babbling in unsynchronised Turkish.

At one end of the couch, where the veranda and the wall of the house makes a corner, a small girl – Beyza – sits with her legs drawn up against her body and her hands clasped around her knees. She is wearing pink shorts and a white T-shirt. Her toenails have been painted bright crimson, her little wrists are hooped with bangles and tiny rings adorn her fingers. She sits with her head resting on the veranda's wooden rail and her thick, dark hair shines in the light from the street lamp. The women know she is pretending not to be there and, for the time being, they pretend not to see her.

Beyza can smell the warm, heavy nearness of the women and is almost reassured. One of them is her mother, the others are her aunts or are cousins of her mother. Many of them are unknown to her. Earlier today an aunt and an uncle that she couldn't ever remember seeing before had arrived in a truck covered in so much dust that she knew they must have travelled a very long way. In the back of the truck was a huge cow's head. It had been skinned but she could easily make out the shape of the big face and was both repulsed and fascinated. Even her aunt's kisses couldn't distract her from it. When her uncle threw the head out onto the road at the side of the house, she sat on the veranda rail and watched her mother pour buckets of clean water over it to wash away the dirt of the journey. It was only then that she began to believe in the party and to feel caught up in the excitement. And it was then that her brother, Ahmet, who had been inside enjoying the attentions of his gathering relatives, had strutted out to the veranda and pinched her arm. Quick as a flash she'd reached around and grabbed a fistful of his hair and yanked it as hard as she could. He yelled and ran back inside the house where the men roared with laughter and she'd heard one of them say, 'She's jealous, that's all.'

She isn't sure why they're having a party for Ahmet but she knows something special is about to happen and that other families are having parties for their sons too. It's something to do with Ahmet being a boy and being eight years old. Beyza is only six and already she has learned when to use anger and when to use charm to manipulate the men in her life. But tonight she isn't quite sure where she fits in to all this activity so she huddles into the corner and lets the sounds seep into her until her mind fills with the chirping of the cicadas in the vines above her and the tones of the women talking.

Ahmet comes out and the women look at his little fat, puffed-out chest and one of them laughs and says, 'Look at the fine little man he is becoming.'

They all laugh. Ahmet is both embarrassed and pleased. He picks up a chilli and throws it at Beyza but she pretends not to notice. Her mother scolds him, 'Leave her alone.'

He sneers at Beyza. She sticks out her tongue at him, daring him to react, but he goes back inside to the men.

The next morning the men take over the veranda while the women cook. A drummer arrives. He is a small, thin man in a brown shirt, old, grey trousers and dusty sandals. He pounds out a steady, mournful beat, on and on without let-up. Beyza's father and two of her uncles appear laden with bottles of raki, which they open and soon all the men are dancing and singing to the beat and the drummer ups his tempo.

Beyza has never seen her father dance and sing so much before. She would like to dance too but some instinct tells her not to interrupt their strange, rhythmic bonding. Ahmet is also watching and drinking from a bottle of Coke. He comes over to her and offers her some but when she reaches for the bottle he snatches it away and laughs. An old man produces two ancient, curved knives and begins to dance, clinking the blades against each other above his head. He dances slowly and solemnly, frowning in his effort to keep his balance. The other men form a circle around him. The drumbeat quickens. The old man dances faster. The knives glint and clash against each other above his head. Beyza looks around for Ahmet but he is nowhere to be seen and suddenly the drumming and the knives and the dancing and the shouts of the men frighten her. She runs into the house to look for her mother and her aunts. A strange figure stands inside the door. He is wearing a white turban and a white, bejewelled suit. Around his waist is a scarlet sash and out of the sash the jewel-encrusted handle of a dagger can be seen. It is Ahmet. Ahmet has become a prince. This is the reason for the party. Why hadn't her mother told her that Ahmet is a prince? This is why he pinches her arms and breaks her toys and pushes her off the veranda so she cuts her knees. A prince can do whatever he likes. Ahmet doesn't even look at her as he strides out. She follows behind with her mother and the other women. A horse has appeared. The horse is also dressed up in jewels and frills. It is a horse fit for a prince. Beyza's father places Ahmet on the horse and the men rush forward and pin money on Ahmet's clothes. Beyza can scarcely believe it. She turns to her mother, 'Is Ahmet going to be rich now?'

'Yes,' her mother laughs. 'Very, very rich.'

They watch as Beyza's father and uncles lead the young, mounted prince away.

It is many hours before they return. Ahmet is smiling the way a prince would smile and his clothes are covered in money. Beyza sits on the veranda rail and watches her father lift him down from the horse. A man in a grey suit appears. He is carrying a large, brown leather bag. Beyza's father ushers the man and Ahmet into the house. The uncles crowd in behind them. Beyza is curious but when she goes to follow them one of her aunts grabs her. The aunt, whose name Beyza can't remember, lifts her up in her arms and carries her across the street to another veranda where her mother and all the other aunts are drinking Coke. Someone gives her a Coke and an ice cream and she is very pleased that her brother is a prince.

Ahmet didn't reappear that day but the drumming and the dancing men continued long into the night. Beyza was fast asleep when her mother carried her off to bed. During the night she awoke and heard Ahmet crying. She could hear her mother murmuring softly to him but she couldn't make out what she was saying.

In the morning all the aunts, uncles and cousins prepare to leave for their own homes. Some of the uncles are very sick and when the aunts laugh at them they growl and hold their heads in their hands. Even Ahmet is sick. Beyza tiptoes into his bedroom and sees her mother bending over him. He is still crying and there is a bloody cloth lying on the floor beside his bed. Beyza wants to go to him and ask what happened but her mother chases her away. Instead, she goes out to the veranda where she sees her father sitting on the couch.

'Did the man with the knives hurt Ahmet?'

Her father laughs, 'No. No.'

'Is he not a prince anymore?'

'Ahmet is a man now.'

She wants to climb up into her father's lap and snuggle in to him and ask him what this means. But her father leans back, closes his eyes and laces his fingers across his stomach and she knows she must not disturb him anymore. She hears her mother call her name. But she is not ready to return to the morning routine of cleaning and cooking. Instead she scampers off to hide in the shade of the olive trees and think over the events of the past days.

When she returns to the house later she is surprised not to be scolded for her disappearance. Maybe Ahmet becoming a man means that her life will be easier now. She climbs on to the veranda rail and watches her mother sweep dust out to the street. Ahmet comes out. He walks slowly and she remembers the bloody cloth. She feels a rush of sympathy for him as he hobbles towards her. Perhaps now she can ask him what really happened. He stops in front of her. She is distracted by a tiny spot of blood on the front of his white trousers. Suddenly he lunges at her, knocking her backwards off the veranda rail. It is only a short drop and her backside cushions her from hurt but, as she sits in the dirt and listens to her mother yelling at Ahmet, she realises that whether Ahmet is a prince or a man will make no difference. Her life will be the same as it always has been.

SPACE-TIME   KEVIN GRAHAM

Beginning with a misread line of Auden's

Warm and still are the lucky skies
of this strange room where life begins
in the peachy light of a lava lamp
and conversation with a stranger.

She puts us both quickly at ease
and fills the screen with your universe:
the planet of your skull a blur
emerging in starry darkness.

I'm floating somewhere in outer space
when the drumbeat of your heart
commands the airwaves
and I'm brought back down to earth

the way a clutter of starlings
investigates a snowy tree,
both our worries going up in smoke
in the titbits of her observation.

THERE'S SOMETHING KILLING ALL THE POETS
MARK GREENE

A poet, widely acclaimed for his sonnets,
has been dispatched into an early grave.

Another – a future laureate – was recently discovered
blue-faced in her attic, hanging from the rafters.

There's something killing all the poets

Some have gone into hiding: a cabin in the Highlands,
a barge on the Avon Ring, the unused office at the library.

Some have taken more drastic steps: a hard-boiled author
of crime noir fiction, hired to investigate the threats.

There's something killing all the poets

Typewriters are being dismantled, laptops are being erased,
recitals unattended and ink not set to page.

The Poetry Society has noticed a sudden drop in membership.
But the police don't want to know; the press don't seem to care.

There's something killing all the poets

And not even their words can save them now

TOO LATE   KEVIN HIGGINS

Every other syllable slashed through
    with a sigh that's a sky
with nothing to say
    for itself but rain, or a child crying
in an outside toilet
    forty years ago.

You now have proof
    they've been plotting against you,
but don't want to give up
    on the old man across the fields
who used to pay one chocolate bar
    per visit, until the oil crisis came
and your voice began to crack.

    Every other syllable slashed
through with a sigh.

    After that, it was just
a shared pack of wine gums
    occasional Sundays,
when there would always be
    a different boy already
taking up space by the fire.

    A sky with nothing to say
for itself but rain.

    Thirty years you've searched
for a girl to take pity
    on a pretend agnostic.

Today, you shuffle up to Communion looking
        like someone who probably
touches himself in the Confessional,
        while thinking about the people
of the Third World.

        A child crying in an outside toilet
forty years ago.

        You pick at your dinner
like a man who knows
        what doesn't go down
the lavatory ends up in a grave
        hardly anyone will visit. Each night
you walk through the firestorms at Dresden,
        asking everyone you meet
for a light.

APPLE BLOSSOM GIRL   FIONA HONOR HURLEY

Apple blossom is blowing in the churchyard again, Megan. The days are brightening, spreading their tendrils into the evenings as dandelion heads poke through cracks in the pavement.

How many years has it been now? Long enough to put grey in my hair and a roll of fat around my middle. Long enough that I'm out of touch and foolish. Or was I always out of touch and foolish?

But I can still remember how you looked as you took refuge from a summer shower beneath the bus shelter. You'd just finished an ice cream and were licking your fingers. The rain pasted your daisy-print dress to you, but your sun-brown legs lead downwards to sandals and pastel-painted toenails.

I offered you the shelter of my umbrella. You ducked in beside me – I was skinny then, my hair still brown – and I could smell warm droplets on you.

'You're a pal, Pete. I hate the rain.'

'When I'm rich and famous I'll give you a lift in my Merc and you won't ever have to get wet.'

'Huh!' You wrinkled your nose. 'I'll be passing you out in my Ferrari by then.'

We were old friends, growing up together on the same street. But something was different now: the way your eyes and cheeks shone, the cling of your dress, the feel of you so close. I felt disappointed when we reached your house, third terrace from the end, the one with the overgrown garden and the unpainted gate.

'Thanks for walking me home, Pete.' You kissed my cheek quickly. 'I'd ask you in, but ...'

'I know.'

Your mum was more than fond of a drink, which made your home so unpredictable that you could never invite friends in. Not even good friends, faithful friends like me. The front door was pale green, number 15. The 5 hung crooked, tilting towards the 1. You disappeared into your house, the door shutting behind you, and I stood for a long time in your wake.

Summer passed into autumn. We took the bus together and got off just before the church, where we threw branches at the apples. Your teeth were white as they crunched the juicy flesh, your cheeks fresh as the fruit. Then you hoisted your bag on your shoulder and we both trudged down the alleyway to school.

I sat behind you, watching you cross and uncross your ankles beneath the desk. Mr Fergusson read a poem while you chewed the ends of your pencil and spat the bits into the disused inkwell.

Then you met James. He had long hair, a pierced eyebrow, and granite eyes. He was a few years older than us and had left school before anybody could remember. He had a shiny red car, which he always kept clean although his fingernails often weren't.

Sometimes you didn't get the bus, because he met you outside the gate in his red car with its plush grey seats. Some days you didn't come to school, and when I met you, you murmured something about 'better things to do'. Things that didn't include me.

Winter drew in, and the trees were black skeletons. You shrank with the day's length; your cheeks lost colour with the sky. You muttered and shrugged when I asked what was wrong. Worse – you avoided my gaze or walked on the other side of the road. A few days before Christmas, I managed to stop you in the corridor.

'How're things?' I asked. Just a normal question, between friends. It didn't sound as anxious as I felt, did it?

'Alright, I suppose.'

'Alan's parents are away New Year's Eve, so he's having a party. Are you going?'

'Maybe.'

There were shadows in your eyes.

'Well.' I swallowed awkwardly. 'Maybe I'll see you there.'

Everyone in our class came to the party. I squeezed through the hallway, pushing and elbowing through the crowds, wishing I was anywhere else. People thronged, three to an armchair, ten to a sofa, twenty to a floor. They crushed peanuts and Pringles into the carpet and threw beer cans in a heap under the Christmas tree. Katie emerged from the bathroom after half an hour, reeking of regurgitated vodka. Alan turned the stereo up so loud that the music's throb vibrated the banisters, the radiators, even the sweating walls.

I was the only person who heard the doorbell. On the step, you clutched the collar of your denim jacket and blinked sleet-flakes from your eyelashes.

'I left James.'

The noise of the party receded as you came inside.

'Let me take your coat.'

We stepped over people on the stairs to Alan's bedroom. I threw your jacket on the bed with all the others, and you shut the door behind you. Downstairs, the music stopped. Five, four, three, two, one ... I kissed you on 'should auld acquaintance', and we sank into the billow of coats.

Damn it, Megan, it should have been our year.

But you never returned to school. I looked in vain on the bus, stared pointlessly at the empty desk in front of me. I asked Katie where you were, and she told me you had gone off with James.

School made less and less sense. I missed you twiddling your hair, crossing and uncrossing your ankles, and shifting in the seat when you grew bored. I twisted a ballpoint pen around my fingers, the teacher's words bumping in to me like driftwood.

Spring came, buds sprouted on branches, and dandelions flared yellow in your front garden. Your front doorbell made no sound – probably broken – so I knocked hard. Thankfully, your mother was sober for a change. She worried a hand through her hair and her eyes were lost as a child's.

'Megan's with James. Yes, I have his address.' She looked at me sadly as she scribbled on the back of an old envelope. 'Pete, there's nothing you can do. I tried ...'

I snatched the paper.

'Maybe I can try harder.'

James's place was in a four-storey apartment block. I pummelled his number on the intercom and he answered through the crackling speaker.

'Who's this?'

Instead of giving my name I demanded:

'Is Megan there?'

Your voice trailed in 'Peter ...' and then was cut off. I thumped the intercom again, and again. I must have got the wrong number at least once, because an old man answered and yelled back at me.

Then I saw your face at the window. You wore a cardigan over your daisy-print dress. You seemed limp as a puppet, and I could just see you mouth 'I'm sorry' before James pulled you away and pulled over the curtain. I collapsed on the cold doorstep, my elbows blocking my ears as a police siren wailed in the next street.

I knew, then, what was wrong. I had seen it often enough, growing up around here, but never thought it would happen to you. I remembered the way you'd let me unbutton your blouse, but wouldn't let me take it off. Because I might have seen the needle marks threading your arms. James was only a cipher; my real rival was not a flesh-and-blood man but a powder that would blow through my fingers. I couldn't fight it any more than I could fight the changing of the seasons.

So what happened, that day in May? Did you misjudge your dosage? Did you finally give up? They found your body in the churchyard, under the apple trees as the first flowers began to bloom.

When I returned to James's apartment, he was reluctant to let me in until I convinced him that I wouldn't hurt him. I didn't come looking for revenge, but to know my rival, to feel the magic powder rush through my veins. I wanted the intensity of a hundred New Year's Eves. I wanted to feel as you had felt, to swoosh through worlds you had lived in, to at last know you, Megan.

I closed my eyes as James tightened the belt around my arm. Soon I would forget everything: the grey streets, the oppressive tower blocks, the dead leaves and empty wrappers in the alleys. You licking ice cream in the rain, your toenails pink and yellow and blue. All would disappear in a haze, dissolve into a vein ...

Then I remembered a vein, the one that ran along the side of your throat. When I had kissed it, your breath slowed and your heart beat faster. Your heart that was now stopped.

My eyes cracked open to see James lift the syringe and pull it slowly back.

I breathed very slowly, and he realised he'd made a mistake in letting me in. We were about the same height, but I was a good deal stronger since my muscles hadn't wasted like his. Although he flailed and kicked I was able to hold his throat long enough to choke the air from him, and I let him drop like a rag doll to the floor.

Too many years have passed, Megan, and not enough to show for them. Behind bars, the days drag too slowly and the years race too quickly ahead. Now the children look away from me as they trudge down the alleyway to school. I am a man with half his life behind him, and the stamp of prison on his face.

I suppose there are worse fates.

The summer air dazzles me with brightness as the dandelion seeds rise steadily to the sky. I stand beneath the apple tree and let the blossoms fall around me, teasing with the possibility of new life. But this is not my season any more. If I close my eyes, I can almost see your glimmering outline, can almost taste your breath. Don't make me open them, not for a while.

THE SCENT OF GREEN   PHIL VERNON

I've all I need: my books, TV, a view
of sparrows and squirrels in the apple tree;
and when they mow the lawn, I almost dare
breathe unlost summers in the scent of green.

Other girls never returned to their life before –
I quietly hid my uniform, away
from where my hands might search the wardrobe rail,
and placed my demob bag in the attic, to fade.

My family welcomed me to their routines,
but the clouds of peace hung heavy on our home
and no-one wanted more for me, nor seemed
to wish me to want more, than I'd once known.

I couldn't wish what they did not, nor keep
my raw imagination under rein:
she flew too fast – and when horizons loomed
she shied, I fell; and never rode again

and half forgot I'd shared a bond, dark hours
and dreams with friends, and helped to win a war,
and danced the conga in Trafalgar Square.
Days pass. In here I'm safe; I'm fed; I'm warm.

A WHIFF OF GRAPESHOT   CRAIG KURTZ

A man will fight harder for his interests than for his rights.

Napoleon is president
and France will be magnificent;
we've had enough of Jacobins,
just wait until the fun begins;
now, sabre-rattling's de rigueur
and trade is less than laissez faire;
the Continental System's what
we'll employ to kick England's butt;
they say that war will be our lot,
just give 'em a whiff of grapeshot;
flag-waving is now commonplace
and Austerlitz the next safe space;
the treaties come, concordats go,
when we want 'facts', we'll let you know;
the Pope, we hear, is quite upset,
that's just so quaint in a puppet;
newspapers harumph, scholars frown,
we'll shut those institutions down;
they say the great mans' staff's corrupt
but, oh!, those buildings going up;
it's all for the good of dear France
(and some ministers of finance);
the soldiers will all lay down their
lives for the Legion of Honor;
we'll rid the streets of criminals,
who needs statutes and articles?;
you're either with us, or you're not,
remember that whiff of grapeshot;

we're going to have progress, my friend,
'tho there's some rights we might suspend;
democracy's the stuff of quips,
reality's more like bullwhips;
Napoleon is president
and opposition's immoment.

DISASTERS   EAMONN LYNSKEY

Poem dedicated to the man who found his car clamped and complained that it was a disaster.

Damocles knew how frail the thread
but Saki caught the sniper's bullet
urging others to be careful

and St Ruth astride at Aughrim,
giving orders, never saw
the cannonball that took his head.

That pleasant Ache afternoon
its people did not understand
the towering wave would overwhelm them

and remember how in Paris
Roland Barthes stepped into traffic,
died in hospital days later?

Tantalus played a cruel jest
but Damocles could see the blade
that dangled overhead, just as

enforcement of the parking laws
is something not quite unexpected,
not completely down to Fate

whereas disasters come to us
unheralded and strip us bare,
are pitiless and coffin-shaped.

THE DUST   MARTIN KEAVENEY

efore light, I rise. I have figs and black coffee in the dark. A dog barks in the street, metal wheels rattle, there are voices in the distance, I shiver in my pyjamas.

I sit up on the mattress, newspapers fall, dust rises, I cough, I suck down on a Sweet Afton, feel the relief. I am ready.

Barefoot on the concrete I get to the hall, down the steps, damp with morning dew, tinge of green from emerging moss, I pull back the bolt, push the door in, straining with its weight, feel around in the darkness, the switch clicks in the weak light, I can see.

He is in the centre of the room. Every day, it is like I meet someone new. The changes are so acute, I am melancholic for his being of only a few days ago, but that manifestation is gone forever.

I go past him to my bench, on the far side and slide on my clogs. I will soon need more dust. The cart passes on Fridays and I try to arrange it so I never run out, but it is not an exact science, there is always the danger.

I half fill a bucket with water, pull out one of the sacks from the press near the door, I score the top with a blade, pour into the bucket. Hills form over the top, I stir it together with a stick, I always enjoy the rippling textures and odd colours that swirl into the water.

As I let it settle, I stand before him, scratching my beard, wondering where to spend the day. I think I lean toward the left leg. I have spent the past weeks around the bottom half. The top is yet a faraway summit, to jump to it directly now might have disastrous consequences for my mood.

It will be shrewder to move up, in the radiance of the final months. For now, in the misery of the early-to-mid point, I decide for this morning at least, to focus on what can be done simply, without ferocious concentration, without danger of excitement or distraction, there are so many already.

I hear another early morning wagon pass by, there is a cry from somewhere, it echoes down the street.

I wipe my mouth, take up a paring tool off the bench. I get on my knees and start to scrape the end, picking up the key at the thigh, careful to go with the grain, it would be shameful to have fractures after all this agony.

The keying takes up most of the time waiting for the mixture to be ready for application, a fortunate quirk of nature.

I try to avoid the loops of meaningless meandering thoughts as I scrape, finding pleasure in the ridges appearing, the flaky flowery shapes scattering to the ground, the smell of freshly hoked mould, my hands becoming workmanlike again, the lethargy dissolving, the body warming, enthusiasm rising.

When the end of the thigh is keyed, I stand back from him. A bell rings from the commercial lanes. It is noisier outside now, the cribs of wagons rattle, bottles clink in crates, horses clip-clop on the cobbles. I go up the steps, my eyes adjusting in the bright slice of sun beaming through an arch across the rooftops. I drink a cup of coffee on the doorstep, watch figures passing by, my buttocks cold on the steps through my pyjamas. I take an Afton from my chest pocket, strike a match, smoke and yawn.

Between two chimneys that shadow me in the moonlight of my late walks over and back across the bridge, my gaze slows on the hands of the tower clock in the town square across the streets. The hands are still but move all the same even as I watch. The mixture has been setting in the bucket for an hour. I toss my cigarette, hurry down the hall, the mug left steaming on the doorstep, my clogs clicking on the concrete.

Downstairs, breath held, I reach for the bucket, poke it with the curved hoking tool. I heave softly, it is just right, the dampness delays the setting process.

I scoop out marbled daubs with a special spoon, agriculturally apply them to the thigh my fine edged tools will refine later. Yet the cleverer I am now, the less paring I will have to do in the late afternoon when my stomach will be rumbling, eager for grilled pig liver and onion, a small bottle of barley wine, an hour or two on the newspapers.

After I apply the bucket, I wash it out in the sink. I take a thin threaded cloth from the bench, unfold it, apply it to the leg, press around the dull shape. I take up a flat-edged trowel to skin off the minute piped rolls that emerge, smoothing the shape to the diagrams from my precious journals. They are permanently banded together in my safe upstairs, the instructions memorised. I would not risk their wafer leaves in this sodden workshop.

I carefully peel the cloth away, the new limb formed a little more. I will be able to sculpt the curve when it has set further, uncover the slight proudness of the veins, the beam of bone, the soft bell of muscle, this requires me to guide one hand with the other, my fleshy actions becoming steadily more mechanical as I progress. Often, when the evening closes in, as I engage the skills I have honed over decades, it is as though something else guides my finishing tools, and I am simply hovering behind, little more than an observer, an Afton smouldering between my lips, a draught breezing through the folds of my pyjamas, my clogs stiff as life on the concrete, the metal wheels, wagons cribs, clip-clop of horseshoes all clattering together on the street outside.

LIFFEY FLOOD   ANNE MAC DARBY-BECK

November 2002

A fall of rain
and we are all at sea;
the city centre creaks
to a damp halt;
like falling dominos
the wave moves outwards
and we are caught
in the bleed of a failing artery;
inching towards the Liffey
empty of traffic,
rows of flashing blue
along each bank.

Black and lemon-yellow
from head to ankle,
a young Garda,
getting dog's abuse
as if this act of God
(or ecological vandalism)
was all his fault;
abandoning decorum,
pulls off his biker helmet,
feet together he jumps
into a pool of mucky water,
splashes, playful as a child.

LUNCH IN THE SKY   CSILLA TOLDY

The Morse tapping of your eye-
lash can move mountains
on the other side of the ocean
or cause a desert storm.

Yet you are sitting like birds on
the crane trying to spy
the crumbs of last night's supper.
Humble and helpless like children

it's hard to believe that these men
built that enormous empire
state building on lunches in the sky,
on air-borne bread and bacon.

In the aftermath of sunset,
the scaffold collapses
and monochrome workers dive bomb
home at last, contented smiles.

IN THE SEPIA YEARS   GERARD SMYTH

... we look completely
different, completely the same
                    Linda Pastan

Here they are in the beginning, in the sepia years.
The first progenitors who look ill-at-ease
in front of the Cyclops eye of the camera,
but still in this image that you hold to the light
you can recognise the resemblance
between those in the picture and your face
in the mirror that has kept a semblance
of the hereditary blueprint that still decrees
a body's strength, a body's weakness;
the shape of shoulders, the first neurosis.
With each new alliance the line continued,
the clan extended: cousins and siblings,
grandparents and grandchildren
carrying within them laws that were written
on the genesis-genes, in the sepia years.

NO REAL PEOPLE   EAMON MC GUINNESS

They were going to call him Alex. It was her grandfather's name. Paul told her it was bad luck to name a child before it was conceived but she said *nonsense, who told you that?* She started painting the back room and wouldn't let it become a dumping ground. *What if it's a girl?* he asked. *Alexia then,* she said, *Alex or Alexia.*

She was told she should try new things, to change her routine, to get out of her head a little. She's been advised to look at the world anew. So she started making small, unnoticeable changes: eating in new restaurants and listening to different radio stations. She's told nobody about this. In chippers she orders bags of chips, tells the cashier she'll be back in a minute and disappears. She waits for buses for half an hour and walks away when they arrive. On her way home from work she avoids the main roads. They're always full of traffic. She goes through the park, estates and back lanes. Her neighbours hardly know her. She's new to the area and has only talked to some of them briefly.

She's started opening windows again: the little one in the bathroom after a shower and the small one in her bedroom when she wakes up. She hadn't noticed that she'd stopped doing it. When they were together they'd wake up, take off the duvet and hang it over the banisters, open the window and let the air in. She bought a clothes horse and a dirty clothes basket. For the last few months she'd been hanging the clothes on door handles, on the backs of chairs or on hangers on the curtain rail. There's something wrong with the final spin of the machine and the clothes come out soaking wet. They leave puddles on the floor. It's on her to-do list. But now she's combining things: the open windows, the washes, the new radio stations and the list. Some things can run parallel again she thinks, some things.

On the weekends she likes taking the bus to areas she doesn't know: Rialto, Perrystown, Drimnagh. It doesn't matter where. She was told to travel in her own city, to see it with fresh eyes; with tourist eyes. On the bus she gives herself little tasks: sit beside someone, even if there are spare double seats, start a conversation, ask people to turn down their music. She likes the idea that people might think she's busy and has somewhere to go. Sometimes she rushes, sometimes she strolls and sometimes she asks directions, even if she knows the way. In town she allows people to stop her: beggars, tourists, chuggers; anyone.

Some days she pretends she can't speak English when people ask her questions. Other times she asks confused-looking tourists if they're lost, then walks them to their accommodation, points out local information and advises them where to go at night. Occasionally she meets them for drinks and tells them lies about herself. She gives a different name each time. She always mentions Paul and Alex. There are no new people, no real people, she thinks. None of them matter.

In May, in the hairdresser's, she told the lady she was going to her son's communion. She enjoyed the small talk and the hands running through her hair. She spoke all about Alex, how he was getting on in school, what hobbies he had and where they were planning to go on holidays. She goes to a different hairdresser's every time.

On the October bank holiday she watched the marathon. She liked cheering on people she didn't know. A woman made small talk.

Are you waiting for someone?

Yeah. My husband Paul, he should've passed by now.

Is he fit?

Quite fit, yeah, he's done it the last two years. Do you know anyone doing it yourself?

Yeah, two friends of mine. One passed a few minutes ago and I'm waiting on the other one.

I hope Paul is alright.

Maybe you missed him. What time is he hoping for?

3.30.

They've passed a long time ago now, you must've missed him.

Maybe. I hope he's alright.

She wants to leave each place cleaner than she found it and take back some control in her life. So in every public toilet she picks up stray bits of tissue paper, collects any rubbish, wipes the seat and mops up piss from the floor. In cafes she always brings her cup to the counter. She craves little touches, is obsessed with them; the cashier in Lidl brushing off her hand when giving change or her Pilates teacher correcting her posture when she makes a mistake. Sometimes she messes up on purpose so the teacher comes over and gently touches her shoulders or back. People patted her arm when she went back to work. Ireland isn't great for touches. No one knows whether to hug or shake hands, especially with women. It's never spontaneous. You can always feel it coming. You see people who haven't met in years, how they sort of dance around touching and it becomes a half-hug half-handshake. That's why she likes going to the continent. There are more rules there.

Only once did she walk near their old house. One Friday after work and she was halfway in the wrong direction when she realised where she was. She kept going for a minute and stopped outside one of the big houses that they used to joke about being able to afford one day. She saw a man playing with his child on the green. She remembered him. She used to pass him every day coming home from work. She'd forgotten about him completely. She wondered about all the people around here she used to nod and smile at. All these people now gone from her life. Where were they? Now she had a new route, new strangers and new houses. But he still had all of this. It was his family home, it was only right that he stayed and she left. But it was their home, for a while. That was what killed her, how he still had the little things he didn't even appreciate, things he didn't even notice, things she craved. He left her with the new when all she wanted was the old.

She notices less and less these days. In the past she'd listen to the sounds of the street. She used to love the energy of the students smoking outside the college building. She'd look at the Turkish men talking in the empty barber's, their hands moving in the air. On the bus she'd take notes into her phone of funny bits of talk she overheard. Paul loved that. But not anymore. She can't retain anything and nothing interests her now. One Friday after work she went to Madrid. She booked a last-minute flight. They'd been there on their second anniversary. In El Prado museum she stared at a painting of a street battle where only the horses looked her in the eye. The description said that it depicted how flawed humans were and how animals were the rational ones. It reminded her of when she went back to work after Paul had left her. No one could look her in the eye.

She always hated him in airports. He's the type who is the first one out of the traps on a plane, standing up in his seat the second they land and taking his bag from the overhead locker when he's not supposed to. Then he has the tag and boarding card binned before leaving the terminal. Nothing is brought home. Nothing lingers. Everything is about moving on, the next thing always. You wouldn't know he'd been away.

He had an activeness that both bored and intimidated her in equal measure. He was always trying to do two things at once. She hated how he crossed the street. He never expected traffic and took it as a personal insult. He walked into the middle of the road, ran in-between dangerous gaps and left her on the other side, making hand gestures to show how slow she was. He was someone who wasn't there. He looked like he could take off and fly. She always felt she was walking up a mountain when walking beside him. But still, she missed him and wanted him back. They used to ask each other how they'd end up, what they'd look like when they were older. Now she sees him in every man. She's become someone new. He has too. He could be anyone. She can't deal with any of them, sees them all as the same.

They tried and tried for a baby. He said he couldn't imagine not being a father. He didn't dump her. He just put her aside until she couldn't find her way back. The details came out slowly. She burst out crying in the office when someone with his name had an appointment. In moments of weakness she told people what had happened but always regretted it after. She stood by him when they thought it was his problem. He didn't when it was hers. The day she heard about his baby was the day she walked home the wrong way.

She started walking to work two months ago. She bought white runners and changes into her office shoes when she arrives. She keeps them under her desk. She used to laugh at people who did that and now she is one of them. Today, like every other day, she walked home slowly, trying to avoid people and the main roads. She was walking through an estate near her apartment when she saw a dead cat lying in the middle of the road. She walked past it, stopped, turned back and stared at it. The right eye was bulging and blood was pouring from its body. With her shoe she scooped it onto the grass verge and kept walking. Nobody else was around. She walked to the main road and sat on a wall. She listened to some songs on her phone and watched an old man move slowly up the street. He was carrying a shopping bag and was almost fully bent over. He needed to stop every few steps to lean against the wall, regain his balance and cough. She started crying.

She wanted to touch him, guide him, help him and do his shopping for him. She imagined the two of them going for a drink afterwards and hearing his life story and she telling him all about Paul, his new baby, the cat, her washing machine and everything else. But she didn't do anything. She couldn't. She didn't move until he went out of sight and into the petrol station on the corner. It had gotten dark and started drizzling. She got off the wall and noticed streaks of blood on her shoe. In the dimming light it could be dirt or a logo. She rubbed it with the sole of her other shoe but it made no difference. She started walking. She thought of the days ahead, how there was nothing she had to do and no one she had to meet. She'd take the bus tomorrow and go somewhere new. Sutton maybe. She'd have to put the runners in the washing machine when she got home. Hopefully they'd be dry by Monday. Wet runners can take ages to dry, she thought.

SEEDLINGS   JEAN TUOMEY

It's not the conversations
we could have had that I regret;
evenings I studied while you worked late,
and we met in the hall, at the table
or on Sunday drives and camping holidays.

It's on days like today,
planting seedlings, red mizuna, kale, beetroot
or soaking the beans we found in the shed
the first spring after you'd gone –
that's when loss sprouts.

A DISTANT ISLAND   DEBORAH MOFFATT

It seems as if the distance is greater now than once it was,
between that island, that little lump of banded gneiss
and vanished trees, and this unsteady shore.

Back when everything was close, I stood in a crowded bus,
flesh pressed against flesh, the hands of strangers
straying over my hips, the warm breath of a whisper
moistening my neck. 'Come,' you said.

It might be the island that is moving further out to sea,
or the shore receding, as if there had been a disagreement,
the one so steady and firm, the other, inconstant.

And now there is only this impersonal distance, a thumb
pressed against the soft resistance of a plasma screen
or a hand splayed over stuttering keys, one finger
hovering, always, over 'delete'.

Or is it that nothing at all has moved, yet the distance
between island and shore has grown: an illusion,
a lack of perspective, a trick of the imagination?

It is too far from me now, wherever it is, that little island
with its memory of trees and its elegantly folded rock.
Only a stray breath of wind can bring you back to me,
and only my faltering hand can breach the distance.

THE DEAD   WENDY MOONEY

They come with great change or after suffering,
their voices calling us, so we jolt awake to hear
our name said in astonishment or quizzically, as if
through the walls of an adjoining room.

Their younger selves in dreams, we suddenly stumble
on them, open doors and there they are
in sunlit spaces with sky or sea for eyes,
discussing ballads, singing, laughing in the world

not ours, eyeing magazines in towns we never visit,
Carrick-on-Shannon, Baltimore or Enniscorthy –
never a wide expanse before them, contained,
looking into, through and past us,

like beautiful uncomprehending dolls
who do not see our urgency, empathise
with our pain – art works, installations
from the outer edges, simulacrums

made of light and air,
telling only of themselves.

The elderly living, almost transparent in the August sun
on the park path below the Dublin mountains
(I see their blue veins through their skin)
remind me that my mother talks to me in dreams

and that I can't remember what she says.
It's understandable: something got smaller,

a person walked away in the distance.
I am not then when I was not: I am now
and again I am now – that is
what it all boils down to.

WAIF, ISMA'IL   ANDREA WARD

My son, I was a poet once, a war ago.
Aleppo was beautiful then, remember.
Arches spanned the narrow coolness of our street.
Our courtyard had a grapevine and a little well.
From my shoulders you reached high to pluck
the sun that fruited in the orange tree.
Now the doors of our house hang open onto ruin.

For two years after you left I went on teaching.
I used to ask my pupils what they dreamed.
One said, 'About my dad. I want him back.'
One said, 'Our house, the way it used to be.'
One said, 'I have no dreams.' Then I stopped asking.
In the street I watched children playing skittles
with marbles and the brass casings of bullets.

Since my brother brought you across the sea
I have no word of you. Against all omens,
my heedless hope is that you are still alive,
my waif, that you have found sanctuary.
Here, in the city that is your birthright,
barrel bombs are falling, our faith is failing.
We were not born to die like this, nor born to kill.

The graveyards have spread out into the hills
but rubble entombs us now, lost multitude.
Rubble has buried your mother and your sisters.
As the first snow sifts down its silent seal
I pray my cloud-flung words will someday find you,
Isma'il Salama, son of Ibrahim.
Remember, I am with you in your blood.

LAST ONE   KARLA VAN VLIET

I held my hands out,
two offerings. If they held

song they held lament,
I say, my hands were a kind

of ladle, immersed and raised up
in sacrament, baptism or Eucharist,

a libation, holy grief, the water
bearing bodies to shore.

Above there is vast blue,
it is all there is, ecstatic blue.

I taste the blue on my tongue,
it tastes of prayer, of inception.

I feel so sad, grief the husk of joy.

Artist's Statement

Cover image: *Hidden* by Maeve Curtis

My practice is sited between paint and photography exploring our metaphysical relationship to technology, specifically image technology. Through media ranging from sculptural installations to paint my work teases out the mysteries and metaphysics that ghost around the invention of photography and plays on a fear of photography that was prevalent amongst the intelligentsia of late nineteenth century Paris, some of whom were convinced that each time a photograph was 'taken', it removed a spectral layer from us. I investigate this anxiety using as my starting point my own family snapshots. Giving consideration to strangers and loved ones alike and equipped with the tools of paint and brush I set out to recover these lost moments of the soul in a gentle attempt to release them into an otherworldly place of arrivals and departures.

www.maevecurtis.ie

Biographical Details

Lindsey Bellosa has had poems published in both Irish and American journals, most recently *The Comstock Review*, *The Galway Review*, *Poethead*, *Flutter Poetry Journal*, *Emerge Literary Journal* and *The Cortland Review*.

Robert Beveridge is a musician and poet. He has recent or forthcoming work in *Dime Show Review*, *Communicators League*, and *Mad Swirl*, among others.

Bruce Boston is the author of sixty books and chapbooks, including the dystopian sf novel *The Guardener's Tale* and the psychedelic bildungsroman *Stained Glass Rain*. His writing has received the Bram Stoker Award, the *Asimov's* Readers Award, a Pushcart Prize, and the Rhysling and Grandmaster Awards of the Science Fiction Poetry Association.

Peter Branson is a full-time poet, songwriter and traditional-style singer whose poetry has been published by journals in Britain, the USA, Canada, Ireland, Australasia and South Africa, including *Acumen*, *Agenda*, *Ambit*, *Anon*, *Envoi*, *The London Magazine*, *The North*, *Prole*, *The Warwick Review*, *Iota*, *The Frogmore Papers*, *The Interpreter's House*, *SOUTH*, *Crannóg*, *THE SHOp* etc. He has won prizes and been placed in a number of poetry competitions over recent years, including a 'highly commended' in the Petra Kenny International, first prizes in the Grace Dieu and the Envoi International and a special commendation in the Wigtown. His last book, *Red Hill*, came out in 2013. His latest collection, *Hawk Rising*, was published by Lapwing, Belfast.

Michael Brown's work has been published widely including recently in *The Rialto* and *Butchers Dog*. He has published two pamphlets, *Undersong* (Eyewear, 2014), and *Locations for a Soul* (Templar, 2016).

Brian J. Buchanan's poetry has appeared in *Modern Age*, *Literary Matters*, *Cumberland River Review*, *Puckerbrush Review*, *Valley Voices*, *Potomac Review* and other journals. His book reviews have been published in the Nashville *Tennessean* and in *In Concert*, the magazine of the Nashville Symphony. He is the former managing editor of the First Amendment Center's website, firstamendmentcenter.org, at Vanderbilt University.

Sandra Bunting has had an academic career at NUIG, has worked in journalism, and as an editor. She is on the board of the Galway-based literary magazine *Crannóg*. Her publications include short stories, *The Effect of Frost on Southern Vines*, a poetry collection, *Identified in Trees* and co-writer of the non-fiction *Claddagh: Stories from the Water's Edge*.

Edel Burke has been highly commended in the Over the Edge New Writer in 2014 for fiction and longlisted for poetry in 2016. She is working towards a first collection.

Jo Burns was one of Eyewear Publishing's *Best New British and Irish Poets 2017*, and has been nominated for a Pushcart Prize. Twitter @joburnspoems

Colette Coen has twice been shortlisted for the Scottish Book Trust's New Writers Award. In 2013 she won the Waterstones Crime in the City Competition and has regularly been published in print and online. Her first novel *All the Places I've Ever Been* and three short story collections are available on Amazon. She has worked as a librarian and a literacy lecturer. http://colettecoen.wordpress.com.

Maeve Curtis is a graduate of the National University of Ireland, Galway and had over a decade long career in corporate management before she decided to study Fine Art. A first class honours degree graduate in Fine Art from the Centre for Creative Practices, GMIT, Ireland, she was awarded the AIB Graduate of the Year in Paint and the Galway City & Galway County Council Emerging Artist Awards in 2007. Selected for numerous juried shows she has also had solo exhibitions with Galway Arts Centre, Ireland (2008) and Norman Villa Gallery, Ireland (2010). Her work has been purchased for private and public collections for the President of Ireland (2008) and Galway City Council, Ireland (2011). Selected for the prestigious Threadneedle Prize, London and the Pallas Periodical Review, Dublin (2011), her artwork was also shortlisted for the Crash Open, London (2012) and for the Thames & Hudson 100 Painters of Tomorrow, London (2013).

Patrick Deeley's poems have appeared widely in journals and anthologies. *Groundswell: New and Selected Poems* is the latest of his seven collections. He has also written works of fiction for young people and his memoir, *The Hurley Maker's Son*, was recently published by Transworld Ireland.

Tricia Dearborn's poetry has been widely published in literary journals and anthologies, including *Contemporary Australian Poetry* (2016), *Australian Poetry Since 1788* (2011) and *The Best Australian Poems 2012* and *2010*. She is on the editorial board of *Plumwood Mountain*, an online journal of ecopoetry and ecopoetics, and was poetry editor for the February 2016 issue. Her most recent collection of poetry is *The Ringing World*, published by Puncher & Wattmann.

Patrick Devaney has published four novels for teenagers and four for adults: *Through the Gate of Ivory*, *Úna Bhán: Flaxen-Haired Rebel*, *Romancing Charlotte* (written under the pen name Colin Scott) and *The Grey Knight: A Story of Love in Troubled Times*. His poems have appeared in magazines such as *Revival, Boyne Berries, Crannóg* and *Skylight 47*.

Chris Edwards-Pritchard's fiction has been published in *Bellevue Literary Review, The Irish Literary Review, Litro*, the Bath Short Story Award Anthology and twice in the Bristol Short Story Prize Anthology. In 2015, he won the Gregory Maguire Award for Short Fiction. and in 2016 he won the TSS International Writers Award and was also runner-up in the *Writers' & Artists' Yearbook* Short Story Competition. His work has been shortlisted for BBC Opening Lines, the Royal Academy & Pin Drop Award and the Colm Toibín Short Story Award.

Jesse Falzoi's stories, as well as her translation of Donald Barthelme's *Sentence*, have been published in American, Russian, Indian, German, Swiss, Irish, British, and Canadian magazines and anthologies. She holds an MFA in Creative Writing from Sierra Nevada College.

Eilish Fisher was awarded a position at the Bread Loaf Young Writers' Conference at Middlebury College Vermont in 1997. She holds a BA in Literature and History, an MA in Irish Literature and a Doctorate in English Literature from the National University of Ireland, Maynooth. She has appeared on academic panels and conferences in the UK and Ireland, most notably the Leeds International Medieval Congress. She is a member of the Irish Writers Centre and the Avoca Writers Group.

Tanya Farrelly is the author of two books, *When Black Dogs Sing*, a short story collection (Winner of the Kate O'Brien Award, 2017) and *The Girl Behind the Lens*, a literary thriller published by Harper Collins. Her stories have won prizes and been shortlisted in many competitions, among them the Hennessy Awards, the RTÉ Francis MacManus Awards, the Cúirt New Writing Prize and the William Trevor International Short Story Competition. Her stories have been widely published, appearing in literary journals such as the *Cúirt Annual, the incubator journal* and *Crannóg*. She has also read her work on RTÉ's Sunday Miscellany. In 2013, she completed a PhD in Creative and Critical Writing at Bangor University, Wales. She works as an EFL teacher and a creative writing facilitator. She co-hosts Staccato Spoken Word night with her husband and fellow-writer David Butler.

Nicola Geddes works as a musician and teacher. She has been previously published in *The Galway Review.*

Sean Gill is a writer and filmmaker who has studied with Werner Herzog and Juan Luis Buñuel, documented public defenders for *National Geographic*, and was writer-in-residence at the Bowery Poetry Club from 2011-2012. He won the 2016 *Sonora Review* Fiction Prize and other recent work has been published or is forthcoming in *The Iowa Review, McSweeney's, ZYZZYVA, Fourteen Hills*, and *So It Goes: The Literary Journal of the Kurt Vonnegut Memorial Library.*

Teresa Godfrey has written five feature-length screenplays and two audio plays on commission and has had two children's dramas broadcast on Channel 4. She was awarded the EU New Media Talent Award for her screenplay adaptation of the novel *Black Harvest* by Ann Pilling and she has been shortlisted for the Orange/Pathe Prize and the Miramax Award. She has won the Allingham Award and her stories and poems have been published in various local anthologies and been broadcast on radio.

Kevin Graham's poems have appeared in *The Irish Times, Oxford Poetry, The Stinging Fly*, and *Crannóg* among others.

Mark Greene is a poet, short-story writer and novelist. He has previously been published in *Now Then, Platform for Prose, STORGY, The Cadaverine, Clear Poetry* and *Ink. magazine.*

Kevin Higgins is co-organiser of Over The Edge literary events in Galway. He teaches poetry workshops at Galway Arts Centre, Creative Writing at Galway Technical Institute, and is Creative Writing Director for the NUI Galway Summer School. He is poetry critic of *The Galway Advertiser*. He has published four collections of poetry with Salmon, *The Ghost in the Lobby* (2014), *Frightening New Furniture* (2010), *Time Gentlemen, Please* (2008), and his best-selling first collection, *The Boy With No Face* (2005), which was shortlisted for the 2006 Strong Award for Best First Collection by an Irish poet. His poetry is discussed in *The Cambridge Introduction to Modern Irish Poetry* and features in the anthology *Identity Parade: New British and Irish Poets* (ed. Roddy Lumsden, Bloodaxe, 2010) and in *The Hundred Years' War: Modern War Poems* (ed. Neil Astley, Bloodaxe, April 2014). A collection of his essays and book reviews, *Mentioning the War*, was published by Salmon Poetry in 2012. His poetry has been translated into Greek, Spanish, Italian, Japanese, Russian, and Portuguese. In 2014 his poetry was the subject of a paper 'The Case of Kevin Higgins, or, The Present State of Irish Poetic Satire' presented by David Wheatley at a Symposium on Satire at the University of Aberdeen. *2016 – The Selected Satires of Kevin Higgins* was published by NuaScéalta in early 2016. A pamphlet of his political poems *The Minister For Poetry Has Decreed* was published in 2016 by the Culture Matters imprint of the UK-based Manifesto Press. His most recent book *Song of Songs 2.0: New & Selected Poems* is published by Salmon.

Fiona Honor Hurley has been published in *Crannóg* and *Number Eleven*, and her articles have appeared on Bootsnall.com and SavvyAuntie.com. https://taleswildatlantic.wordpress.com

Martin Keaveney has had fiction, poetry and flash published in Ireland, the UK and the US, in *Crannóg, The Crazy Oik* and *Burning Word* among others. His play *Coathanger* was selected for development at the Scripts Ireland festival in 2016. He has a BA and MA in English and is currently a PhD candidate at NUIG.

Craig Kurtz versifies Restoration plays. Excerpts appear in *California Quarterly, Dream Catcher, Papercuts* and *Penn Review.* http://antickcomedies.blogspot.com/

Eamonn Lynskey is a poet and essayist. His third poetry collection is *It's Time,* (Salmon, 2017) *www.eamonnlynskey.com*

Anne Mac Darby-Beck writes poetry and short stories. She has had work published in such magazines as *Poetry Ireland Review, Cyphers, THE SHOp, The Interpreter's House* and others. She has won several awards including first place in Syllables Poetry Competition.

Eamon Mc Guiness has had poetry, fiction and memoir published in *Boyne Berries, Looking at the Stars, Skylight 47, Abridged, The Honest Ulsterman, The Galway Review, Bare Hands Poetry, The Bohemyth* and *Wordlegs.* He has been shortlisted for the Strokestown International Poetry Prize and for the Cúirt New Writing Poetry and Fiction Prizes, the Penguin/*RTÉ* Guide short story competition and longlisted for the Over the Edge New Writer of the Year Award. He has recently completed an M.A in Creative Writing in U.C.D.

Deborah Moffatt won the WOW award for poetry in 2015, and the Wigtown Poetry Competition (Gaelic section) in 2015 and 2016. She has published one collection, *Far From Home* (Lapwing, 2004), and is currently working on a collection of poems in Gaelic. She lives in Scotland.

Wendy Mooney has previously been published in *Poetry Ireland Review, Crannóg, Windows Publications: Authors & Artists, New Irish Writing* and several other journals.

Robert Okaji is the author of three chapbooks, his work has appeared or is forthcoming in *High Window, Boston Review, Into the Void, Taos Journal of International Poetry & Art, West Texas Literary Review,* and elsewhere.

Linda Opyr was the Nassau County Poet Laureate 2011–13. She is the author of seven collections of poetry and her poems have appeared in numerous anthologies, journals, magazines and newspapers, including *The Hudson Review, The Atlanta Review, The Paterson Literary Review,* and *The New York Times.* She was the Visiting Poet in the 1999–2000 Writers Series at Roger Williams University. She has been featured in the 2012 Walking With Whitman Series and the 2002–03 Poetry Series at Long Island University, the C.W. Post Campus; and has served on the poetry faculty of the New England Young Writers' Conference at Bread Loaf. In April 2001 the Suffolk County Legislature presented her with a Proclamation for her work. She holds a Doctor of Arts degree in English and American Literature from St John's University. She was a featured poet in the Bailieborough Poetry Festival in 2017. She lives on Long Island, New York.

Csilla Toldy's poems have appeared in online and print magazines such as *Poetry Monthly, Snakeskin, Fortnight, Lagan Online, Sarasvati, A New Ulster, The Honest Ulsterman, Poethead.* She has a chapter of poetry in *Mothers and Sons: Centering Mother Knowledge* published by Demeter Press, Canada. She has two poetry chapbooks published by Lapwing Publications Belfast, *Red Roots – Orange Sky* and *The Emigrant Woman's Tale.*

Madelaine Nerson Mac Namara's work has been published in *Southword, THE SHOp, Crannóg, Cyphers, The Cork Literary Review 2016,* and in *The Deep Heart's Core* anthology (Dedalus Press, 2017). She was guest reader at Ó Bhéal, Cork, 2016. Her first collection *The Riddle of Waterfalls* (Bradshaw Books, 2015) was shortlisted for the Strong/Shine Awards 2016.

Jessamine O Connor facilitates The Hermit Collective, and the weekly Wrong Side of the Tracks Writers. She recently won the *Poetry Ireland* Butler's Cafe Competition 2017, previously won the iYeats and the Francis Ledwidge awards, and has been shortlisted for several more including the Hennessy and the Over The Edge New Writer of the Year. She judged the New Roscommon Writing Award 201 and the 2017 Roscommon Poets Prize for Strokestown Poetry Festival. Three of her chapbooks are available from www.jessamineoconnor.com. A fourth is published by Black Light Engine Room Press and was launched at the Crossing the Tees Book Festival in June 2017.

Knute Skinner's collected poems, *Fifty Years: Poems 1957–2007*, was published by Salmon in 2007. A limited edition of his poems, translated into Italian by Roberto Nassi, appeared from Damocle Edizioni, Chioggia, Italy. *Help Me to a Getaway* – a memoir (2010), and *Concerned Attentions* – poetry (2013) appeared from Salmon. His latest collection, *Against All Odds*, was published by Lapwing in November 2016.

Gerard Smyth has published ten collections, including *A Song of Elsewhere* (Dedalus Press, 2015), *The Fullness of Time: New and Selected Poems* (Dedalus Press, 2010) and *The Yellow River*, a collaboration with artist Seán McSweeney (Solstice Arts Centre, 2017). He was the 2012 recipient of the O'Shaughnessy Poetry Award presented by the University of St Thomas in Minnesota and is co-editor, with Pat Boran, of *If Ever You Go: A Map of Dublin in Poetry and Song* (Dedalus Press) which was Dublin's One City One Book in 2013.

Jean Tuomey facilitates writing groups in Mayo and trained as a writing facilitator with the National Association for Poetry Therapy in the USA. She is published in *Crannóg, Fish Anthology, Stony Thursday* and *Washing Windows*.

Phil Vernon's poems have appeared or are forthcoming in *Other Poetry, Ink Sweat & Tears, Elbow Room, Gold Dust, Pennine Platform* and the *Kent and Sussex Folio*. He has been shortlisted and commended in various competitions, most recently in the Shepton Mallet Festival and the Out of Place poetry and music collaboration. https://philvernon.net.

Karla Van Vliet is the author of two collections of poems, *From the Book of Remembrance* and *The River From My Mouth*. She is an Edna St. Vincent Millay Poetry Prize 2016 finalist and was nominated for a 2015 Pushcart Prize. Her poems have appeared in *Poet Lore, Blue Heron Review, The Tishman Review, Green Mountains Review, Crannóg* and others. Her chapbook *Fragments: From the Lost Book of the Bird Spirit* is forthcoming from Folded Word. She is a co-founder and editor of *deLuge Journal*, a literary and arts journal, as well as the administrator of the New England Young Writers' Conference at Bread Loaf, Middlebury College.

Andrea Ward has worked as a secondary teacher of English and Art in Ireland and South Africa. She has published articles and book reviews in educational and theological journals. She is a contributor to RTÉ's *Sunday Miscellany*.

Ali Znaidi is the author of several chapbooks, including *Experimental Ruminations* (Fowlpox Press, 2012), *Moon's Cloth Embroidered with Poems* (Origami Poems Project, 2012), *Bye, Donna Summer!* (Fowlpox Press, 2014), *Taste of the Edge* (Kind of a Hurricane Press, 2014), and *Mathemaku x5* (Spacecraft Press, 2015). He lives in Redeyef, Tunisia. aliznaidi.blogspot.com.

Stay in touch with Crannóg @ www.crannogmagazine.com

Lightning Source UK Ltd.
Milton Keynes UK
UKOW03f1500040617

302606UK00002B/66/P